SAPPHIRE

DAUGHTERS OF THE DAGGER SERIES - BOOK 2

ELIZABETH ROSE

ROSESCRIBE MEDIA INC.

Cover created by Elizabeth Rose Krejcik

Edited by Scott Moreland

ISBN: 13-978-1500815691

PROLOGUE

ENGLAND, JULY, 1356

*L*ady Sapphire de Burgh from Blackpool lay beneath her husband, the Baron of Lydd as he parted her legs and plowed into her as if he were doing naught more than planting a field.

She closed her eyes and tried to drift to her secret place she'd always disappear to when the man came to claim his husbandly rights. She'd only been married to the baron for two moons now. Two moons too long in her opinion. And while she had originally been betrothed by her father to Lord Roe Sexton, a man she'd never met, that is not who she'd ended up with as her husband.

To her dismay, when she'd arrived in Rye eagerly antici-pating her marriage, she'd been informed by Roe Sexton's uncle that her betrothed had died while campaigning in France for King Edward III. And she'd be marrying the visiting Baron Walter Poussin from Lydd instead.

She should have known from the moment she'd seen the beady-eyed cur that her marriage would be one of hell, and not a marriage of love. She'd been hoping for a marriage of love after seeing how happy her sister, Ruby was with her new husband. And Ruby was due to have a child by the end of the year, which filled Sapphire with even more longing and anticipation. Sapphire loved children and wanted many of her own, with a loving man to have sired them. That dream had been dashed the day she'd married the baron.

While Sapphire was only nine and ten years of age, her new husband was over forty. He was overweight, balding, and had a nose on him twice the size of what lay beneath his belt. He was crude, punishing, and hadn't an ounce of manners in his entire body. He was the saddest excuse for a lover she'd ever seen. Or that she ever imagined, since she'd not had a lover before him.

"Open wider," he snarled and belched in her face.

She had to obey for fear he'd beat her the way he did the first time she'd objected to coupling with him. Squeezing her eyes shut, she counted the thrusts. Sixteen, seventeen, eighteen – the man was so predictable. She tried to picture that secret garden in her mind but couldn't. Then she tried to pretend he was someone else, but that just didn't work either.

He huffed and puffed above her and on the twentieth thrust she thanked God that it was over. She lay still upon the bed and watched him collapse into a drunken stupor next to her. Only when he started snoring did she let out a breath of relief.

Then she ran to the washstand and cleansed her body of this filthy man. She scrubbed with a cloth between her legs and took a deep breath as the friction brought her to life. Oh, how she wanted to feel the ecstasy and excitement her sister, Ruby, had told her one felt in the throes of passion and in the midst of coupling. She'd even heard the idle chatter of the kitchen servants speaking of their heightened pleasures and satisfaction as well.

They all enjoyed coupling with their mates. They looked forward to it every night. Instead, she prayed each night she'd die in her sleep rather than have to satisfy her husband again.

As she sank to her knees in front of the hearth, the fire-light danced in patterns on her full, bare breasts. Her body was in the prime of her youth, and it would please any man as well as bear many children. However, neither had happened with the baron. He'd told her if she didn't conceive soon, she'd be of no use to him at all.

Sapphire wasn't in love with the man, but she was in love with the idea of birthing children – many children and someday being a mother. Sadly, she was starting to realize this marriage would not bring any of her dreams to fruition.

Feeling sad and lonely, she was physically, mentally, and emotionally unsated. Sapphire was married now, but being a woman, she also had her need for release. It mattered not. In order to achieve that, she had to touch herself to bring about the desired outcome. But it just wasn't satisfying enough. She needed a man. She needed a husband who would be gentle with her and not raise a hand to hurt her. She wanted someone with manners who cared for her and with whom she could feel safe in his protective arms. She wanted a lover who could please her, as well as a man with whom she could raise a family. Sapphire needed to feel alive and be respected, not worthless and be treated worse than the castle's stray hounds.

Hugging her legs, she glanced back to the bed where the

monster roared in his sleep. Then she focused her gaze on the dying embers of the fire. She picked up her nightdress from the floor where her husband had thrown it when he ripped it from her body. As she tossed it into the fire, she watched the flames ignite.

That would be her soon. Her flame would ignite also. Things would change and she'd find the happiness in her life she'd dreamed about since the day she saw her mother's undying love for her father give her one last reason to smile before her life drained from her body trying to give the man the son he'd always wanted.

Her parents had been in love. And though she was only four years of age when she'd lost her mother and baby brother as well, she'd never forget the bond her mother and father had shared.

She'd find that bond and happiness with a man someday, but it wouldn't be with the man she'd been forced to marry. If it was the last thing she ever did, she'd also find that pleasure she'd heard whispered about on the tongues of sated lovers. In need, she would go out and find a man who would love her, caress her, care for her, and sate her desires, even if her soul would burn in hell from being unfaithful in her loveless marriage.

The man she'd dreamed of was nothing like her husband. Mayhap, she decided, 'twas because he was a noble that cared only for titles and riches and naught of love between a man and a woman. The same was true of most nobles. Perhaps her parents and sister were the only exceptions.

Her mother had believed in true love, and that's why she'd named her children after jeweled daggers bought from a blind hag. 'Twas a superstition that they'd find true love brought on by their mother's actions. Unfortunately, her father discarded of the daggers when he lost her, saying they were cursed and to blame for her death. Now, without the daggers, Sapphire wasn't ensured true love in this lifetime at all. But she wanted it so badly, that she would now do whatever it took to fulfill her dream – and her mother's dying wish – be it immoral or deceitful, she no longer cared. She wanted love and she wanted to feel sexually sated, too. If that made her an evil person – then so be it.

Mayhap, she decided, she needed to look toward the commoners for her answer. The nobles didn't seem to be able to give her what she needed. Aye, she decided, she'd start her search in a common place amongst simple people. Mayhap that is where she'd find the answers for this thing called love.

CHAPTER 1

LATE SEPTEMBER, 1356

*L*ady Sapphire pulled the hood of her mantle lower to hide her face as she entered the Bucket of Blood Tavern behind her stableboy, Dugald. She shouldn't be in town this late at night and amongst commoners, but she was trying to escape her husband, Lord Wretched. That is, the baron. People had no idea what a horrible man he really was. And if he found out she'd ever been here, he'd take his fist to her, she was sure.

Sapphire only wished the marriage had not been so rushed, and that her father and sisters could have been present. Perhaps her father would have stopped the marriage, since the baron was not an original part of the negotiations he'd made with Roe Sexton's late father, Robert, who died just before her arrival. But she'd been convinced by her dead betrothed's uncle who was also Robert's brother, Lord Henry Sexton, that this was the proper thing to do and not to jeopardize the alliance between Blackpool and Rye. Therefore, Sapphire did the deed, to ensure safety to her father's lands, and especially for the safety of her younger twin sisters, Amber and Amethyst, back home.

She didn't regret for a moment coming to the Bucket of Blood Tavern, searching for answers. After all, there was nowhere else to go since her own bed was occupied with one of her husband's latest women. Since he found her body not planted with his seed, his impatience won out and he went on to sample any woman in the castle he could get his hands on. Still, none of them had been impregnated by him.

She was grateful he hadn't touched her now in over two months, because she wanted nothing to do with the vile man ever again. No woman would ever bear him an heir no matter how many he sampled. God was punishing him for not only bedding every woman in the castle – be she a noble or merely a servant – but also for beating the women when they did not conceive. She'd had her share of bruises from his punishing hand, and knew this is not what she should encounter in a marriage or coupling.

She stopped in the doorway, glancing at the patrons in the dimly lit room. The Bucket of Blood Tavern was a favorite gathering place for sailors and fishermen since it was so close to port. With Rye being one of the Cinque Ports, she realized she'd find many honorable men here who had vowed to protect the channel for their king. Men of the sea filled the tables and wooden benches, also standing at the drink board that served as a counter. The innkeeper handed them ale, wine, brandy, and drinks of many kinds, in tankards made of metal or wood. Each cup had a large curved handle on the side. Women of the night clung to the men, wearing their low-cut gowns, working the room, and trying to earn a living.

The large burly man guarding the door, the bouncer, held out his hand and growled in a low voice.

"Ye know the charge. A hay-p'ny from each o' ye. Now pay up."

Like most taverns and inns, there was a petty charge at the door to cover any damages of broken bottles or benches should a patron get rough. And in a place like this, chaos was always evident.

Sapphire slipped two halfpennies to the boy, and Dugald handed them over to the bouncer. The man held out his board of wet wood and, one at a time, bounced the coins atop it to make sure they were real and not made of lead. Satisfied, he nodded and grunted.

"Go ahead," he said, stepping to the side, enabling them to enter.

She followed Dugald forward into the room, stepping carefully atop the dirty rushes spewed across the floor that looked and smelled as if they hadn't been changed in years. She wondered what rancid scraps of food or how much spittle lay hidden beneath them.

Sapphire felt nervous, yet excited at the same time. 'Twas far from proper to be sneaking out of the castle and coming here in disguise, but she just had to feel alive outside the clutches of her doomed fate. She'd convinced the stableboy to help her sneak away and to bring her to the tavern that also served as an inn. He'd even supplied the commoner's gown she now donned to protect her identity.

Dugald fancied the innkeeper's daughter, Erin, so when Sapphire offered to pay his entry fee, he'd been more than happy to help her. She'd been here half a dozen times in the past two months, always staying in the shadows and watching, letting Dugald talk to the girl who was his own age of six and ten years. While Sapphire was only a few years older than them, she'd always had the nurturing aspect of a mother. And while she wasn't the eldest of her siblings, she'd still acted the part of mother to each of her three sisters through the years.

It was a joy getting away from the castle and out amongst people who were more interesting in her opinion. She needed this in her life right now. And so Dugald kept Sapphire's secret and she kept his.

Sapphire wandered over to the side of the room and slipped into the shadows, trying not to be noticed. Surveying everyone having a good time, she only wished she could join in on the merrymaking. A minstrel played a lute in the corner with a bard singing out the stories of his travels. Men played cards and gambled coins atop the trestle tables. And they all drank. There was laughing, lots of laughing, as the girls teased the men and the men grabbed them for a kiss or just pinched their bottoms. She watched the lovers disappear one after another up the stairs to the second level, sneaking away to have a tryst. They were coupling and though the girls did it for coin, at least they seemed to enjoy it, as they always had smiles on their faces. So did the men.

She felt an emptiness gnawing deep inside her heart, wanting to know enjoyment and pleasure from coupling with a man. But Sapphire's marriage to the baron had proved to be uneventful and unfulfilling in every way. Somewhere along the way in the past few months, she'd started to lose her dream of being happily married to her true love and having a large family, and this bothered her more than anything. She wasn't one to give up her dreams easily, even when times got rough.

She wondered what it would have been like if her original betrothed, Roe Sexton, had not died overseas. Mayhap she could have enjoyed being married and making love then. And mayhap she could have had children, the thing that meant the most to her in all the world.

"There she is." Dugald's green eyes lit up as he spied Erin wiping a rag over the counter at the back of the room. Sapphire felt sadness inside her soul, pitying herself, but yet was happy for the young boy. He had been a good friend to her ever since she'd arrived in Rye. And just in the past few months, she'd witnessed his growth spurt, and now he was even taller than her. He had beautiful red hair and his face was covered in freckles. He was a nice boy, and any young girl should be happy to be in his presence.

"Go to her." Sapphire smiled, knowing Dugald wanted to be with Erin yet felt it his duty to stay and protect the lady of the castle. Never before had he left her out of his sight on these visits, but tonight would be different. The boy deserved some time alone with the girl. Everyone deserved a tiny bit of happiness once in a while. Dugald was more than a boy, as he was a man now. She would give him the opportunity he needed. Hopefully, at least he would have the chance of finding true love, even if she would never know it in this lifetime.

"I'll be fine, Dugald. Go." She turned him gently toward the girl. "Just take your time with her, don't hurry."

"But m'lady –"

Sapphire hushed him with a finger to her lips. "Please, Dugald, don't call me that here." Her eyes scanned the room to make sure no one heard him. "Tonight, I'm just another commoner," she reminded him softly.

"Of course, I forgot, my la–" Dugald stopped himself from using her title, and Sapphire smiled.

"I'll be waiting for you out in the stable. I'll go check on our horses," she told him.

Dugald nodded his head and disappeared into the crowd. Sapphire pulled her cloak closer around her as she felt some of the patrons' eyes upon her. There was no one here for her, she sadly realized. No one that was any different than what she'd left back at the castle. These men were all looking for a whore to satisfy their itches. And satisfied they'd be, and she was happy for each and every one. But she knew not a one of them would ever be able to tell her anything about true love.

"Wench, come give me a kiss."

When one of the dockmen well in his cups looked in her direction, she knew 'twas time for her to leave. The men hadn't bothered her before now because she'd always been with Dugald. Tonight was different. She was alone and fair game for any sex-starved man that saw her as a cure to his problem. Though she wanted to feel the ecstasy of making love, it would not be here and with one of these men.

She was headed for the door when one of the drunken patrons grabbed her by the sleeve and spun her around.

"Where are ye goin' so fast?" the man asked.

She frantically scanned the room for Dugald and noticed him disappearing out the back with Erin on his arm. It was too late for her to call out to him to help her. Besides, he would never hear her in this madness.

"Let go of me, you swine."

She tried to shake the man's grip from her sleeve when

one of his friends came up and grabbed her from behind. His hands snaked around her hips as he pulled her closer.

"Stop it!" she screamed, jumping away from him, but the men only laughed.

"Tryin' to play hard to get, whore? Well, how 'bout three on one? I think the French have a name for this game."

Just then, another filthy man with blackened teeth and rotten smelling breath stepped in front of her and started to undo the tie on his hose. Her heart beat furiously and her eyes opened wide. The other two men decided to grab her by the wrists, not enabling her to move.

Sapphire now realized she'd been wrong in allowing Dugald to leave her side in a place like this. If only she had her sapphire dagger that her mother had given her as a child. If so, she could protect herself the way her sister, Ruby, had done, by killing a man in self-defense. She hadn't even her regular dagger or eating knife at her waist, as she'd changed in such a hurry that she'd forgotten them back in the stable at Rye.

The door swung open at that moment and a group of boisterous, noisy knights entered, cheering and shouting and sounding very drunk.

"Go on in, Sirs," said the bouncer. "No charge fer the nobility, as always."

"We beat those damned French at Poitiers," one called out, handing the bouncer a handful of coins anyway. The man greedily shoved them into a pouch at his side without bothering to bounce them on his board.

"Ground them into the dust, we did," another knight shouted to the crowd. "You should have seen it. We were drastically outnumbered, and still managed to come out victorious in the end."

"Let's hear it for the longbow," shouted an archer who'd entered with them. His hand lifted in the air with a longbow held high for all to see. The crowd cheered and shouted their praises.

"Hold on," said another, raising his hand to silence the crowd and regain their attention. "The best part is that the Black Prince captured their king and his son and is holding them for ransom. King John the Good is not faring so good anymore, I should say."

That sent everyone in the room into a joyous frenzy. They whistled and shouted. There was much backslapping and playful shoving that followed as the knights congratulated each other. Several of them tossed coins atop a table and emptied their pouches to display jewelry – some of the great bounty they'd plundered when they'd defeated their enemy across the channel.

A tall, dark, handsome knight wearing a torn and dirtied tunic beyond recognition over a covering of chain mail, stopped just inside the doorway. He was one of the victorious warriors who'd just helped win the battle at Poitiers for King Edward III. He looked weary, yet still held an air of importance about him. A mustache and beard covered his face. Long, black hair lifted with the autumn breeze blowing through the open door as his blue eyes swept the room and settled upon her. He was a very handsome man, indeed.

She pulled once more against the hold of the men detaining her, trying to free herself and make it to the stable. "Let me go," she shouted.

"Release her," ordered the dark knight standing in the doorway. It was only two words, but words that had her captors obeying. The men took their filthy hands off of her and went back to their prospective whores who awaited them in every corner.

She looked up to her mysterious savior, their eyes interlocking, and she smiled and nodded slightly to show her thanks.

"Welcome back, milord." The innkeeper rushed to the door with a tankard of ale in his hand. He handed it to the knight and half-bowed before him. "We thought ye'd been killed campaigning in France. Ye've been gone a long time and we all thought –"

"Well I'm back now, so stop with the idle chatter. I want a room and a whore for the night. Do you have what I need?"

"Aye, milord. The room at the top of the stairs is free," said the innkeeper with a nod of his head toward the stairway. "And ye know ye're always welcome to pick any of m'girls that ye take a fancy to."

His eyes scanned the room and Sapphire just stood and stared, mesmerized by his domineering presence. He was rugged and handsome. Exciting in a raw sort of way. Yet he held a regal air of nobility about him. This man was a warrior and a protector of her country. He was a brave knight who risked his life for others and was well respected. And he also just protected her from her attackers. Why couldn't she be married to someone like this instead of what she'd gotten?

As he walked over to her, several whores rushed up trying to gain his attention. He ignored them, his eyes still fastened upon her. Sapphire felt a flush of heat surge through her body when she realized he was staring at her. She lowered her gaze and looked to the ground.

He stopped right in front of her, and she had no chance to even think of what to do. He reached up and, with a flip of his hand, he pulled the hood from her head, causing her long, brown hair to spill forth. Sapphire gasped and her hand flew to her hood to try to once again mask her identity, but he grabbed her wrist and looked her in the eye.

"I'll take her," he said in a low voice, still holding on to her. The whores grumbled their disappointment and hurried over to the other men who'd just returned from war. The knight started for the stairs, pulling her along with him before she could even react.

"I'm not available, my lord," she told him, using her free hand to pick up the end of her cloak so she wouldn't trip, moving so quickly through the crowd.

"I pay twice as much as anyone here," he said without even looking back at her. He made his way up the stairs with her in tow and his tankard of ale gripped tightly in his other hand.

"Nay! You don't understand," she said frantically, meaning to explain, all the while watching her path as she climbed the stairs quickly after him.

"Nay, *you* don't understand," he answered, reaching the top of the staircase and kicking open the door to the bedchamber, all but dragging her inside. In one motion, he pulled her to him then and kissed her, sending her head spinning from the surprise and the excitement of his action. Then he released her so quickly that she stumbled backward. Tripping on her cloak, she landed on the bed made from a single stuffed straw pallet, lying directly on the floor. With the air knocked from her lungs, she found herself trying to regain her breath so she could speak.

The knight kicked the door shut, all the while never spilling a drop of ale. "I never get refused. I realize you're new here, as I haven't seen you before. But you need to learn your position."

The room was small, dank, and musty. The only furnishings consisted of a pallet, a small table with a washbasin of water, and a chair. Several hooks lined the wall, and old, broken, wooden shutters squeaked as they moved back and forth from the breeze coming through the open window. It was dark, and the room was lit by only one tallow candle, burning the animal fat quickly in a bowl next to the bed. But even in the semi-darkness, she could make out what he was doing. He removed his scabbard and sword and threw them on the bedside table. Next, he then removed his tunic, chain mail and undertunic, hanging them on a wall hook. Afterward, he sat on the chair and untied his boots.

Who was this man that he thought to even speak to her in this manner? He angered her and she could not let him go on with this, even if he didn't know better and she was still in disguise.

"I believe, Sir Knight, that 'tis perhaps *you* who needs to learn *my* position." Sapphire had every intention of telling him she was a noble and not a whore, but stopped abruptly, distracted by his next actions.

His boots were off and he stood up, causing her eyes to focus on his broad, bare chest. His upper arms were strong with corded muscles and his chest cried out for her to touch it. She shook the illicit thought from her head, watching intently as he drained the ale before slamming the tankard down onto the wash table. In one move, he slipped out of his braies and hose and walked over to the bed stark naked.

"Any position is fine with me. I'm game for something new. Now take off your clothes, wench."

"I will not!" She hugged her mantle closer as she surveyed him.

A muscle in his jaw twitched and he took a step into the candlelight. The man was devilishly handsome. His body alone was a work of art. So unlike her own husband's balding head and bulging stomach. Sapphire bravely let her gaze roam down his strong chest to his taut stomach and to the arrow of dark, crisp hair that led to the biggest interest she'd ever held in a man. He stretched toward her, hard, hot and ready.

Pushing upward on the bed, she meant to say something, but wasn't able to find her voice. Instead, her eyes drank in his perfect manly beauty and she couldn't help but wonder what it would feel like to make love with a man like this. A voice inside her head warned her to get away fast. But instead of listening to her head, she listened to her heart and stayed there, wondering what was going to happen next. Scared, but curious, she allowed herself to tarry just a moment longer. He leaned toward her, kneeling one muscled thigh right next to her hand.

"As you can see," he said, his voice dripping with lust, "I haven't lain with a woman for some time now and am not interested in playing games at the moment."

"I . . . see," was all she could say as her eyes were transfixed below his waist. Never in her life had she dreamed a man could be so ready. She'd never seen the likes of this. Feeling her inner core stir, it made her wonder just what he would feel like against her skin – and inside her body.

She released her grip on her mantle, burning up with the sudden heat in the room. If she didn't remove her cloak soon, she'd melt. Unclasping the brooch that secured her cloak, she let it slip from her shoulders onto the bed in a heap.

"That's better. Mayhap you just need a little help disrobing."

"I'm not a whore," she blurted out.

"You wear the scarlet color used to identify women of your profession," he told her. "So please, stop your little game. I am in great need of your services right now."

He reached out and pulled the leather ties that held the bodice of her peasant's dress together. It was her disguise when she came to town that she'd worn to save her identity. Unfortunately, she hadn't realized until he'd just pointed it out, that it was scarlet – the same color worn to identify whores. No wonder he thought she was one of them. She should have specified to Dugald before he secured it to get her any peasant gown but scarlet. He'd most likely gotten the garment from here to begin with. Too late now, she realized.

"I'm . . . I'm not what you think," she said, licking her dry lips, which only caused him to misinterpret her thirst for a wanton action instead.

"You're right. I don't buy the modesty act. It doesn't fit you." He freed her breasts and ran his hands over them, brushing his thumbs over her nipples, causing them to tighten. She sucked in a breath, her eyes wide since she couldn't believe what was happening. Before she even had the chance to respond, he lowered his mouth to her, fastening his lips around one nipple at a time, sucking her into his warm mouth, using his tongue to tease her.

Sweet Jesu, it felt wonderful, and she noticed an instant tingling between her thighs. So this was what her sister had spoken of feeling with her husband. Sapphire's body never responded to the man she'd married at all, and she had started thinking there was something wrong with her. Then again,

Lord Wretched had never taken the time to do anything like this.

The knight continued his exploration. Sapphire basked in the amount of erotic stimulation she was receiving. Though it was immoral and shameful, it was also wonderful and amazing all at the same time. Her head dizzied. She reached out and gripped his hair, trying to push him away, but found herself too weak and wanton to do it. Aye, she liked this, and wondered if she'd burn in hell for her actions just by enjoying the act.

"I like your breasts," he said, his eyes fastened on them, making her heart thump even louder within her chest.

It was like an icy winter slowly melting into a puddle under his warming summer touch. She tried to speak but couldn't. She struggled, trying to regain her composure.

"They're so full and beautiful and just longing to be tasted." He laid her back on the bed and she found herself unable to object. Her body tingled in places she never knew existed. It was need that made her want to discover more of this enjoyable feeling.

This is what she'd been waiting for her entire life. She was a woman with needs, same as a man. This stranger was making her feel more alive beneath his touch than she'd ever felt before.

He cupped his hands over her breasts, caressing them gently at first and then a bit rougher. As he straddled himself atop her, she wasn't able to look away from what dangled between his legs. By the rood, she was going to hell for enjoying this, and she felt as if she no longer even knew herself. She could feel his warmth and hardness as his tip teasingly rubbed against her groin, right through her skirts.

Panic suddenly ripped through her at the thought of how close they were to coupling. She had to leave at once. Struggling to push upward on the bed, he leaned over her, keeping her in position.

"I liked the taste of your lips, too." His mouth descended upon hers again as he brushed his lips past her in a brief kiss. "You taste good. Like mint. Not like ale and the other foul things most whores taste like. And you smell like . . . rose water?"

"I told you," she said through ragged breathing, trying to ignore her body's cry to couple with this man. "I'm . . . not . . . what you think. I'm . . . I'm a lady." She raised her chin and waited for his reaction. She figured he'd jump off of her now, realizing his mistake. But instead, he grinned from ear to ear.

"Of course you are, and I'm the King of England," he said with a chuckle. "You do amuse me with this coy little game you play. I'll tell you, it truly excites me even more. I've never bedded a tart that toyed with me only to arouse me, and then kept acting like a shy virgin. I like that. But I assure you, I need no more arousing, as I am more than ready."

His tongue shot out and traced her lips. Her mouth opened to tell him she wasn't lying, but his kiss deepened. His tongue invaded her mouth in thrusting motions that had her hips involuntarily imitating the same movement below him.

"Are you ready to please me now?" he asked.

His words echoed in her ears and she found herself repeating them out loud. "Are you ready to please me?" she repeated his words, but he thought she was matching him with the same question.

"Well, I've never been said to leave a woman wanting for more once she's been with me."

He was bragging she figured but, at the same time, she wondered if it were true. She burned with desire beneath her skirts, and needed release as desperately as he did at this moment. She had a yearning to know how pleasure through coupling felt. Her body vibrated beneath him, driving her mad. All she could think about were the passion and ecstasy she'd heard other women speak of when they'd told tales of making love.

Then the most brash, reckless thought entered her mind of going through with the act. Although it should have horrified her, it oddly didn't.

'Twas not an accepted act of a noblewoman, and she could be punished severely if caught. But she no longer cared that she was a lady about to give herself to a man she didn't even know. He excited her in a way that she'd always dreamed of someday experiencing. Sapphire wanted pleasure and satisfaction, and after tonight, she'd never see him again. Afterward, she'd be back trapped in the castle as naught more than a prisoner being wed to a tyrant who thought only of his own pleasures. Her wretched husband would probably beat her once again if he'd discovered what she'd done.

One too many times, she'd given of herself to gain nothing in the exchange. This time, she knew 'twould be different. This was what she'd been waiting for all her life.

He lifted her skirts with one hand and caressed her naked bottom. Men loved the fact most commoners wore nothing beneath their skirts. They were easily accessible that way. She'd gotten used to this way of dress when her husband insisted she be ready for him whenever and wherever he should decide to take her, and burned all her undergarments and hose when she'd tried to defy him by wearing them.

The knight rubbed his fingers over the juncture of her thighs, making her open wider for him. She let out a small moan when she felt a ring on his finger. The friction of the metal against her excited her even more.

Closing her eyes, she threw back her head. He was there again, kissing her lips as he fingered her beneath her skirts. Her body warmed and tingled. She could hear the sound of her own liquid passion as he slipped his fingers in and out.

She moaned, her head thrashing back and forth upon the pallet beneath her. Her knees spread wider as she accepted his advances, and she felt herself wondering why this knight would think to pleasure a woman that he thought was only a whore. Even when coupling for money, he seemed to want to please the woman as well. She could see now why any of the girls downstairs would be first in line to give their services to this knight. Never had she felt so alive. Never had she felt so good. And never had she ever wanted a man the way she did right now. "Please . . . I want you . . . all of you," she found herself saying before she could stop herself.

"That's what I like to hear from my girls. But I don't give you what you want until you give me what I want first."

What kind of game was this man playing with her? Couldn't he see she was at the brink of losing control? Why was he waiting? She wasn't used to this teasing, nor did she think she could endure it even for another minute.

"Anything," she answered in a breathy whisper, watching the rise and fall of her own breasts which only excited her more. Her naked body and his naked body were pressed together. She didn't even know the man, and neither did she care. What could be more exciting?

"Your name," he said. "Give me your name, as I haven't seen you here before."

"That's because I don't come from these parts," she told him.

He removed his hand and she clamped her knees tightly around it in a silent gesture of begging him to come back to her.

"I like to know my partner's name so I can ask for her again if she so pleases me."

By the rood, why was he doing this to her? She had half a mind to tell him her name just so he wouldn't leave her squirming on the bed. But she couldn't. She couldn't let him know her true identity. If word got out she'd been with a man at the Bucket of Blood Tavern, her name would be sullied forever. Besides, her husband would take his hand to her behind and probably punish her by taking her every hour of the day. Still, she needed to tell this man something or she may never find out what it was like to couple in ecstasy and find release.

"My name is . . . Lark," she lied. She didn't know where that came from nor did she care at the moment.

"Lark," he repeated, nodding in satisfaction. "It fits you well. Now, my sweet little bird, I will hear you sing with passion."

She felt worse about lying than she did about what they were about to do. He then lowered himself, gently pushing into her, and she had a sharp intake of breath at the size of him.

"Can you handle me?" he asked.

"Of course I can." She hadn't the slightest idea if it were true, as he was more than twice the size of the baron. Still, she couldn't have him leaving her now, so she'd said what he wanted to hear.

"Are you sure?" he asked almost as if he truly cared. Why should he even ask this if he thought her to be a whore? He was most polite in bed.

He started to move slowly at first until she got used to the rhythm. It was like a dance, a beautiful dance that she never wanted to end. They moved together, meeting each other and she could feel him reaching all the way to her very soul. This is what coupling was supposed to feel like. She now knew what the women in the castle meant when they said they enjoyed it. She understood how Ruby felt when she said it was exciting and vibrant. His hips moved faster and so did hers. Her sensations grew stronger and the tinge of guilt that had first been there was long gone. She felt herself climbing to a height she'd never experienced before, all because of this wonderful man who was taking her on the journey.

The door opened and a whore and a drunkard stood there watching them for a mere moment. She didn't care and the knight atop her didn't seem to notice. She lifted her hips to his and screamed out as she reached her peak. The couple disappeared and closed the door behind them.

He was holding out for her, she was sure of it. And he kept going until she'd screamed out yet again. She wanted more. She couldn't get enough and didn't understand it at all.

He then rolled to the bottom, pulling her to the top. Sapphire felt so free without his restricting weight upon her and her hips moved in a new rhythm altogether. She watched his eyes squeeze closed as her loose hair hung around him. She almost felt like an animal the way she used him for her own needs, cooing and purring like she'd never done before.

She'd risen to her height yet again before he totally let loose. He rolled back atop her and had his way.

She felt him then – the full length of his male hardness. And as he growled with desire, she felt she'd indeed pleased him as much as he'd pleased her. He exploded inside her, causing her to become even more excited, though she didn't think it possible. The thought filled her head that she'd now take with her a part of him to dream about when she returned to the castle. Even if she didn't know the man's name nor would she ever see him again, part of him would still be with her. He would occupy the wonderful memories she'd have for the rest of her life.

The man collapsed beside her and fell instantly into a slumber. Sapphire felt like she wanted to stay there in his arms and wake in the morning to do it all again but knew she couldn't. Dugald would be looking for her out in the stable and be worried, wondering if he'd done the right thing by leaving her.

So she slipped from the man's embrace and gently kissed him upon his forehead.

"Thank you," she whispered and hurriedly dressed. "You've given me something no one has ever given me before."

When she opened the door to leave, she heard the deep timbre of the man's groggy voice from the bed in the darkened room.

"Lark. Where are you going? I haven't paid you yet."

She smiled and answered. "Oh, yes, you have. More than you'll ever know." Then she left, closing the door behind her.

CHAPTER 2

$\mathcal{L}$ ord Roe Sexton rolled over in the bed, smelling the alluring essence of the woman that he'd coupled with last night. The morning sunlight glared in through the open shutters of the upstairs room of the inn, and he squinted his eyes and rolled back the other way.

Lark, she'd said her name was. He'd been away for over a year now, but remembered no commoner with this name in his father's village. He then remembered she'd told him she wasn't from around these parts. He'd have to ask the innkeeper, Auley O'Conner, where he could find this girl. The sweet taste of her still clung to his lips and the smell of roses permeated the stale bed linens. Her long, mahogany hair had been so shiny and clean and her eyes such a bright blue that he couldn't stop thinking of her.

He rolled over toward the pillow she'd laid her head upon and buried his face within it, groaning at the feel of need throbbing once again below his waist. He had to have her again. He'd never been so satisfied with a woman and he'd never known a whore who'd been so clean and refreshing.

She'd told him she wasn't a whore but he knew better. Any girl that entered the Bucket of Blood Tavern, save the innkeeper's daughter, knew what they were getting into beforehand. She'd called herself a lady. Hah. No lady would ever set foot anywhere near such a place. If she did, she certainly would never be called a lady again.

His hand slid under the pillow as he sprawled out over the bed. He stopped suddenly when his fingers brushed across an object. Pulling it out, he adjusted his gaze. It was a small golden brooch used to pin closed a mantle. It was embellished with a crest upon it. He wondered if it belonged to Lark. He sat up in bed and inspected the brooch closer, his vision still blurry from sleep. 'Twas gold, he was sure of it. And 'twas a woman's piece of jewelry. The only women who graced the Bucket of Blood Tavern were poor. This belonged to someone with money.

He raked his fingers through his long, tangled hair and then smoothed down his mustache in thought. Jumping from the bed naked, Roe walked over to the window to inspect it in the light. He could see it better now, and he didn't like what he saw. 'Twas the crest of a deer, its antlers wrapped in vines, its hoof upon a fallen bear.

It was his crest! His father's crest. What in God's name was going on here and how the hell did this whore get a hold of a brooch with his crest on it? Something wasn't right, and he was going to find out what.

As he splashed the cold water from the basin onto his face, he reveled in the way it shocked him and brought him back to life. He'd been away too long and had a nagging feeling in his gut that he should have come home sooner.

As a vassal of the king, he'd only been expected to serve

forty days' service to the king per year. But in times of war, it was determined as needed. For the past year, he'd been traveling at the king's son's side. He followed the Black Prince as he'd tried to instill fear and doubt into the minds of the French that King John the Good could not protect them. And so they'd pillaged, plundered and burned their way from Bordeaux through the Pyrenees to Toulouse, then back through Carcassonne and Narbonne until they once again resided in Bordeaux. Though he didn't feel good about the ways of war, he was proud to say he was part of the victory that took place in Poitiers.

He'd been amongst the army that was outnumbered six to one, when the Black Prince's archers rose in fame to help win the battle and enable the capture of King John and his son.

But he tired of fighting and was home now. Roe needed to, once again, be aware of all that went on in Rye.

He hurriedly pulled on his clothes and boots and strapped his scabbard to his waist. He then held his sword up high to reflect the sunlight that streamed into the room from the window. This sword had been his grandfather's. 'Twas the sword that saved his grandfather's life many times during the Crusades and the only reason Roe was home now instead of dead on the field with crows pecking out his eyes. His father had given it to him when he left even though Roe had felt wrong in taking it. He had a feeling his father needed it now, and he only hoped he wasn't too late.

Roe made his way down the stairs, his head throbbing all the while. On his journey home, he'd drunk heartily upon the ship, celebrating their victory as they made their way over the channel and back home to Rye.

The Bucket of Blood Tavern was to be his last stop before

returning to see his beloved mother and also his father. He could have made it to his father's castle last night but he wanted to be fresh when he saw the man again. He'd had a quarrel with him before he left, not wanting his father's brother, Henry, to make residence at Castle Rye. He didn't like, nor did he trust the man. He only hoped now he could make amends with his father and, hopefully, convince him to send Henry on his way, if he hadn't already left.

"Auley?" Roe called out to the innkeeper as he pulled up a stool and sat near the drink board. The man was nowhere to be found. "Auley, where are you?"

Roe rubbed his hands over his face, trying his best to wake up while he waited for the innkeeper. Being impatient, Roe got to his feet, making his way behind the counter and pouring himself a mug of ale. He surveyed the condition of the tavern from last night's celebration. He'd have to make sure to slip Auley a few extra coins to make up for the shambles caused by his men. However, the innkeeper never was one for cleanliness and, for all Roe knew, it could have looked this way since he'd left.

After Auley's wife left him and moved to Dublin, the man's life seemed to go downhill. Actually, she was never his wife. The woman had been a whore who worked for him. Even after she got pregnant, they'd never married. She birthed the baby but wanted naught to do with it so Auley raised his child by himself. If it wasn't for his daughter, Erin, Roe was sure Auley would have crumbled years ago.

Roe raised the mug to his lips and turned back toward the empty room. Erin stood there watching him, but turned her head away quickly to clean a table when he glanced in her direction.

"Erin?" he asked, picking up his mug and walking toward her.

"Aye, milord." She didn't turn to acknowledge him. Something was amiss. She was a young, blond girl with small features but a large smile.

"'Tis been a while since I've seen you. Turn and face me."

She did so reluctantly, but kept her eyes toward the floor. He'd known Erin since she was a child. She'd never been afraid to look at him before. She was like a sister to him. The sister he never had. He'd had a younger brother, Richard, but he died from the plague that raged across the entire nation eight years ago, taking with it nearly half the population. But surely in his absence of just over a year, Erin couldn't have changed to this extent.

"What possesses you?" he asked. "Cannot you bear to gaze upon my ugly face?"

She smiled slightly and he felt better. He'd always had the ability to make her smile. Reaching out with his finger, he raised her chin to see her face. Her eyes opened wide in fear and she turned away, but not before he could notice the purple bruise staining her cheek.

"God's eyes, what happened to you?"

"'Twas her lover." Auley answered as he descended the stairs. He was small in stature, with light, curly hair and bushy brows. Behind him followed a whore Roe had been with himself once or twice. She winked at him and disappeared into the back room.

"Her lover?" Roe couldn't believe little Erin had a lover. True, that at her age, most noble girls were already married, but the commoners normally couldn't afford marriage until they were much older. Still, one didn't need to be married to enjoy an occasional romp in bed. He looked back toward her and realized he'd mistaken her for a girl when she really was a young woman. Her breasts were trussed up in her bodice and her hips now had a new curve he hadn't noticed before. She'd grown from a girl into a woman in a matter of a year's time. Or perhaps he'd just not noticed, as he always thought of Erin as a child.

"That's right, her lover," Auley repeated. "The fickle stableboy who comes from Castle Rye."

"My father's stableboy? Tell me which so I can have him flogged for his behavior upon my return. I will not tolerate a man lifting a fist to hurt any woman."

"Nay!" cried out Erin. Her father's eyes bored into her and she stopped from saying more.

"The boy's name is Dugald," said Auley. "He has the nerve to come in here with his own whore to begin with. Yet I didn't say a word, m'lord, knowing he came from yer demesne. But when he then saw to bed my own daughter right out in the hay of the stable –"

"Dugald? With a whore of his own?" Roe laughed and took a swig of ale. Dugald was just a lean boy with no experience at all. He couldn't see the boy even knowing what to do with a whore, let alone attract one. And to beat his fist into a young girl's face? Not like the Dugald he remembered. Things were definitely different than when he left, and he didn't like it at all.

"I'll handle this matter." Roe drained the mug and set it on a table. He pulled a coin from his pouch and laid it next to it, then added a few more to the pile. He'd done well with the spoils of war and didn't mind helping out the innkeeper.

"Nay, milord," begged Erin. "Please don't hurt Dugald."

Her father's eyes bored into her again and, with a shake of his head, he silenced her. She liked Dugald. Roe could see that. She wanted to protect him. He didn't understand any of this, but things would change now that he'd returned.

"I'll just speak with the boy," he answered, and Erin seemed relieved. "Now tell me, who is this whore he travels with?"

Auley stepped forward, giving his daughter a slight shove, aiming her toward the back room.

"She's the whore ye bedded last eve, milord."

Roe's heart beat faster at the mention of Lark. He'd find out just exactly who she was now. Mayhap Auley knew where to find her.

"What do you know about her, Auley?"

"Naught, milord. Only that she's – different. I don't even know her name or from where she comes."

"Different? How so?"

Auley picked up a rag and swiped it over the counter. "She covers up with that cloak while the rest of the whores are taking clothes off."

"Where can I find her?" Roe needed to know.

"Don't know, milord."

Roe felt his blood stir just thinking about last night. He hadn't had his fill of the woman yet. He had to see her again. She held some sort of power over him and he couldn't explain it. She'd attracted him like a bee to a flower. He had to know more about her.

"I'll just ask Dugald," he told him. "I'm on my way now to my father's castle. Mayhap my father will even know the whore of which you speak."

Auley stopped wiping the counter and twisted the rag in

his hands. His brow was furrowed and lines creased his forehead.

"I don't think yer father will be able to help ye, milord."

"Why not?" Roe felt his stomach clench even before Auley answered. He knew something was wrong, as he could feel it deep inside himself. He prayed his father hadn't taken ill again to one of his spells. If his father had been ill while he'd been away, he would feel horrible.

"Answer me, Auley. Why won't my father be able to help me?"

There was a moment of uncomfortable silence before the short man answered. It was a silence that would stay with Roe and haunt him for the rest of his life.

"Because, milord," answered Auley with a slight shake of his head, "yer father is dead."

CHAPTER 3

"*L*ady Sapphire, wake up."

Sapphire rolled over in the hay of the stable and opened one sleepy eye. Dugald shook her and looked down at her, the first rays of sun shining around his body from the opened door.

"Dugald?" She sat up and tried to get her bearings. Then she realized that she'd slept in the stable last night rather than to have to go to her solar and sleep with her wretched husband who was entertaining another woman in their bed. After she'd changed back into the gown of a lady in the stable where she'd hidden her clothes, she'd hurried back to her own bedchamber. She'd stood outside the door last night, hearing the noises from within. That's when she decided she would not sleep with this man ever again, even if she were married to him.

"Lady Katherine has been looking for you all morning. Your husband is angrier than a mad hornet that you didn't come back to the bedchamber last night," said Dugald.

"I will never sleep with that vile man again," she retorted, standing up and brushing off the hay from her blue velvet gown.

"What happened last night at the tavern?" asked the boy, going over to one of the horses and brushing it down.

"I met a man, Dugald. A knight." Sapphire smiled and nodded her head, remembering the pure bliss she'd shared with this stranger. "A wonderful knight."

"I know how you feel," said the boy. "I shared a wonderful night with Erin as well. We made love. Did you make love with the knight, too? After all, I heard he took you up to one of the rooms."

"Dugald!" exclaimed Sapphire in surprise. "That is not a proper question to ask a lady."

"Many pardons, m'lady. I didn't mean to pry."

"Please do not say anything about this to anyone."

"Don't say anything about what?" came a voice from the door to the stable. Lady Katherine, Lord Henry's wife, walked in with her long russet taffeta gown trailing behind her, making her look like a queen. The woman was tall and had dark hair coiled around each ear. A golden caul, or hairnet, encircled each braid. It was all secured by a jeweled metal circlet around her head. A short veil trailed down the back of her. She was one of the most beautiful women Sapphire had ever seen. And one of the kindest as well. She reminded Sapphire of her own mother whom she missed dearly.

"Excuse me, m'ladies but I need to be getting to Lord Henry's side to tell him his horse is prepared for his morning ride." Dugald headed toward the door of the stable.

"First tell me what you were talking about," said Lady Katherine, causing Dugald to stop and turn, shifting nervously from one foot to the other.

"He was telling me I shouldn't have been sleeping in the stable," said Sapphire, picking a stray piece of straw from her shoulder and throwing it to the floor. The floor was covered with straw that was used to walk on, as well as for the animals' bedding. Hay was used to feed the livestock. "That's all. Now go on, Dugald. You don't want to keep Lord Henry waiting."

The boy bowed quickly and took off at a run, only too glad to be leaving here right now. Sapphire was glad for the boy's departure as well, since she didn't want him spilling any secrets.

"You are a horrible liar," remarked Lady Katherine. "I know you went to town with the stableboy last night in disguise. I saw you leave, though you didn't think anyone noticed."

Sapphire froze, not knowing what to say. She'd been discovered and this could only mean trouble for her.

"Sit down," said Lady Katherine, settling herself atop a wooden bench in front of a horse's stall and motioning for Sapphire to join her. "Your secret is safe with me, dear."

"Oh, thank you so much," she said, settling herself on the bench and reaching back to pet the horse on the nose. It tried to nibble at her since she smelled like hay. "If my husband found out, he would beat me again."

"Again?" asked Lady Katherine, her brows dipping and her mouth turning down into a frown. "Sapphire, darling, are you telling me that he's hurt you or raised a hand to you on other occasions?"

"On more than one occasion, my lady. And only because I could not bear him an heir."

"That wretched man," she said with conviction. "I told

Lord Henry not to let him marry you, but he insisted 'twas for the best. No wonder you sleep in the hay, my dear. I don't blame you for not wanting to be anywhere near him."

"He takes many women to his bed constantly, and beats them all when they do not conceive."

"I will have to see about this matter. However, my husband is fond of the man and I fear he'll do naught to stop it."

"Wife!" came a bellow from the doorway. Sapphire's heart jumped when she realized the baron stood there with a scowl on his face. She gripped Katherine's hand tightly for support. The woman patted her hand with hers in a reassuring gesture, and then got to her feet.

"Baron Lydd, what brings you to the stable this early?" asked Lady Katherine, walking over to meet him.

"I come looking for my wife who has not been to my bed at all last night." Sapphire could see the anger in his dark eyes. Her body tensed. She highly anticipated another bruise or two coming her way from his iron fist. Still, she would not crumble in his presence, but instead she would be strong.

"I found it hard to do so, my lord, when our bed was already occupied with one of your latest follies," she spoke up bravely, hoping she wouldn't regret this action later.

"You dare speak to me that way?" he asked. "I will take the back of my hand to you if you say another word about it."

"Let her be!" Katherine stepped forward to block him from Sapphire.

"Get out of my way, woman," he snarled. When Katherine stood her ground, Sapphire knew she was in for trouble. The baron grabbed hold of Lady Katherine's arm and threw her to the ground.

"Nay!" shouted Sapphire, meaning to rush forward to help

her. But before she could, a silhouette of a man appeared in the doorway illuminated by the sun from behind.

"Stop!" The man pulled his sword from his side and rushed forward, holding it to the baron's neck. "I should kill you right now for even touching my mother."

"Roe?" Lady Katherine pushed up from the ground and started crying. "Roe, is it really you, Son? I thought you were dead."

Sapphire looked at the face of the man who'd entered the stable, and her heart stopped for a beat. There, holding his sword against the throat of her husband was none other than the knight she had coupled with at the Bucket of Blood Tavern last night. And to make matters even worse, Lady Katherine had called him Roe – her son.

Sapphire froze, unable to move. This was the man she was supposed to marry. Roe was the man to whom her father had betrothed her. Tears welled in her eyes, and she turned away before he could see her face.

"What's going on here?" Lord Henry Sexton rushed into the stable next, followed by Dugald.

"HELLO, UNCLE." Roe kept the tip of the sword steady at the baron's neck as he greeted his uncle with merely a glance. He was glad he'd made it to the castle just in time to save his mother from being beaten by a cur he was ready to kill.

"Roe?" asked his uncle, sounding surprised to see him. "What are you doing with your sword to the baron's throat?" Henry Sexton was a tall, gangly man, with a long nose and a high forehead. He had dark hair, like Roe's father. And though he was the younger of the brothers, the man was already graying at the temples. He wore a dark green gypon with golden buttons down the front as well as down the long sleeves that covered his knuckles. And while he looked the part of a noble, Roe knew the man could never measure up to his departed father.

"He pushed my mother, and he shall pay for this with his life," Roe ground out.

"Nay, lower your sword. Katherine is my wife now, and I shall not hold the baron responsible for his actions."

"*Your* wife?" Roe lowered his sword, not from want but out of shock. Shaking his head, he could hardly believe what he was hearing.

"Roe, your father died six months ago," his mother explained, standing and coming toward him with outstretched arms. "And when you didn't return in over a year, we thought you had died as well."

Roe embraced his mother in one arm, his sword still gripped in his other hand. His mother's tears fell quickly, and she buried her face against his chest.

"I am saddened by the death of Father," he told her. "I only wish now that I had returned sooner. I'm sorry, Mother, but I was in the service of the king."

"Oh, Roe, you should have sent word you were well and alive," she told him through sobs. "And then I would have known where to find you to tell you that your father was sick and dying."

Roe realized his mistake and would regret it for the rest of his life. He should have dropped the grudge against his father and returned sooner. Now, he'd never see his father again, and this disturbed him deeply.

"How did he die?" he asked his mother in a low voice.

"My brother was always sickly, you know that, Nephew," said Henry. "His heart was weak and so was his mind."

"Father might have had a weak heart but there was naught wrong with his mind," Roe disagreed. Of course, then again, mayhap he was wrong, since his father did keep Henry at the castle and that was a bad decision, even if the man was his own brother.

"He made some wrong choices," said Henry. "But I was sure to correct them. I have been in charge of Castle Rye since his demise."

"I see," said Roe. "I also see you've wasted no time in marrying my mother, hoping to gain control of the entire estate."

"I thought it best for your mother to have someone to look after her," said Henry, coming to his side.

"And I see how well you are doing that," Roe answered sarcastically. "I return to find a man raising his hand to her and yet you stand there and tell me not to kill the bastard!"

"This is Baron Walter Poussin from Lydd," said Henry. "He has been living here since he married Earl Blackpool's daughter."

"Your father made the alliance with Earl Blackpool before he died," his mother told him. "Lady Sapphire was to be your betrothed, Roe. When you didn't return, we thought you were dead. Henry decided 'twas best to wed her to the baron and keep alliances with not only Blackpool but Lydd as well."

"*My* betrothed?" Roe asked in surprise, having had no idea of his father's plan. "Well, it doesn't matter. I will choose my own wife and make my own alliances. I am the sole heir of my father's estate, so you can step down now, Uncle. I have returned. And Baron Lydd, you will collect your wife anon and go back to your own castle. If you aren't gone come morning, I will see to it my sword pierces your neck for having raised a hand to my mother."

"I'm sure the baron meant your mother no harm." Henry walked over and stood next to Baron Lydd. "But if you really want him to leave, then I am sure he will abide by your wishes instead of causing trouble."

He gave the baron an odd look that Roe could not decipher. Then the baron straightened his clothing and nodded.

"Of course, I will leave come morning," he said. "Come, Wife!" he called, looking to the other side of the stable.

Roe hadn't even known anyone else was inside the stable since the woman hadn't come forward or said a single word the entire time. He thought it odd the baron's wife didn't go to her husband as ordered. But if the man took to beating women, he could see why the girl was hesitant.

"Sapphire, you need to go with the baron now and ready yourself to leave for Lydd tomorrow," Henry talked to the woman in the shadows.

Slowly, she stepped forward. Roe strained his eyes to see the face of the girl who was supposed to have been his. As she walked into the beam of sunlight streaming into the stable, the first thing he noticed was her bright blue velvet gown trimmed in gold. Her long, mahogany hair fell in gentle waves around her shoulders like a cascading waterfall, all the way down to her waist. She was petite, but had some very alluring feminine curves.

The sunlight illuminated the top of her head, but she kept her face turned toward the ground. Roe was curious and needed to see whom his father had meant for him to marry. Was she fair and comely, or did she have the face of an aged wild boar? Either way it no longer mattered because she'd already been given to the wretched baron. He pitied the poor girl to have to be married to a man who obviously thought naught of raising his fist to her whenever he pleased. Roe would never do that to a lady. He felt guilty that he was sending her away with the man, but he had no choice.

"Raise your face and greet my nephew before you leave, Baroness," his uncle told the girl.

Then, ever so slowly, she raised her chin. Roe's jaw dropped as he saw her bright blue eyes and delicate features. He realized immediately he was looking upon the face of his lover from the tavern last night.

"Lark?" His throat tightened and he didn't understand this at all. The woman he'd spent the best night of his life with was not only the baron's wife, but also the woman who should have been his wife all along? Life had just dealt him a wicked hand and he didn't like it in the least.

"What did you call her?" asked the baron. "You sound as if you know my wife. Sapphire, have you been with this man? Because if I find you have cuckold me, I swear you will pay for your illicit act once we return to Lydd."

Roe saw the fear in the girl's eyes as she first looked at her husband, and then her attention darted back to him. Their gazes interlocked and a tear lodged in her glassy eyes. She silently begged him to keep her secret. Roe couldn't tell them she'd been with him last night, or the baron would beat her and mayhap even kill her. Nay, he couldn't allow that. It was all too obvious now that he'd made the biggest mistake of his life by not returning from overseas sooner. This woman could have been his wife! Sapphire, they'd called her, and he knew she was a real gem. He didn't know what was going on here, but he had to find out before he let her go anywhere with Baron Lydd.

"Nay," he said, softly, shaking his head. "I am mistaken. My apologies, Lady Sapphire." He released his mother from his hold and replaced his sword in his scabbard. Then he walked slowly toward the girl and took her hand in his. "I am happy to make your acquaintance, Baroness." He raised her hand to his mouth and pressed his lips upon it in a slight kiss. "I only hope you can forgive me for having confused you with a girl that I know is naught but a whore."

CHAPTER 4

Daughters of the Dagger

*S*apphire fumed at the knight's words and pulled her hand out of his grip. How could he say she was a whore after the wonderful, passionate night of making love they'd shared together? Suddenly, her image of him changed. He didn't seem so chivalric after all.

"Please refrain from putting your lips upon my hand, Sir Knight," she retorted. "I would not want to be thought of as a wanton woman."

With his blue eyes the color of a summer sky fixed on her, she could see he wasn't amused by her words.

"Well, I once had a woman named Lark who reminded me of you. And I assure you, she was very good in bed, and also very wanton."

She felt her face flush and looked at her feet since she could not look upon his handsome face. Not after knowing what they'd done, and with her husband standing right there. If the baron had any idea, she would be beaten for days when they returned to Lydd.

"Is this some kind of game you play with my wife?" asked the baron. "Because I don't like it, Sexton."

Roe turned to face the man. Sapphire watched as he rested his hand atop the hilt of his sword in a subtle reminder to him of his threat.

"I have reconsidered, Lydd. I would like you to stay on at Castle Rye for a while after all. Perhaps I've misjudged you," said Roe.

Sapphire didn't believe a word of what he was saying. Especially since he'd only changed his mind when he knew she was the baron's wife. Still, she was happy that she wouldn't be leaving with the vile baron after all.

"Good choice," said his uncle happily. "After all, you have just arrived and need time to get to know the baron before you can judge him."

Sapphire saw a vein throbbing in Roe's neck and had the feeling he was biting back his words. Either way, she was happy that she'd be staying after all. She had no intention of leaving with the baron and would do anything at all to save herself from his clutches.

"Well, I think we should have a feast to welcome home Roe," said Henry.

"I'm sorry I won't be able to join you, but I have business in town all day today." The baron excused himself and left the stable in a foul mood.

"Roe, I am so happy to have you home," said his mother, reaching up and pecking him on the cheek. Sapphire felt a tinge of envy. She wished her mother were still alive so she could get a kiss from her as well.

"Come along, darling," said Henry, holding out his arm to his wife. "Roe, are you coming as well? You have missed a lot since you've been gone. I'd like to tell you of the happenings in the past year."

Roe glanced back at Sapphire and answered without looking at his uncle. "I'll be along momentarily," he said.

"Sapphire?" asked Henry. "You need to get to the kitchen and direct the servants in preparing the feast."

"I'll go to the kitchen instead, darling," said Roe's mother, escorting Henry toward the door. "I am sure Sapphire and Roe might like a minute to get to know each other."

"Well, I suppose," Henry said, looking back over his shoulder as Katherine rushed him away.

Henry and Katherine exited the stable. Dugald who'd been standing there so quietly that she'd almost forgotten about him, came forward.

"Welcome back, my lord," said Dugald with a large grin.

"Dugald." Roe put an arm around the boy's shoulders. "I have just come from the Bucket of Blood Tavern and Auley O'Conner tells me you've been with his daughter."

"Oh!" The boy's face darkened. "I am sorry, my lord, but . . . but . . ." He looked to Sapphire for help.

"'Tis my fault," she said. "I asked him to take me to the tavern in secret. If I hadn't, he never would have been with Erin."

"I don't mind the fact you may be sweet on her," said Roe, "but I hear you've hit her as well."

"Hit her?" The boy's eyes widened and his body stiffened. "I would never hurt Erin. I love her." His hand flew to his mouth and he covered it, having spilled his secret.

"I'm willing to bet you bedded the girl as well."

"Lord Sexton, please do not punish the boy," begged Sapphire. "He cannot help the way he feels for the girl. I

47

admire him that he has found true love and I beg you not to put an end to the boy's happiness."

"True love?" He turned and faced her then, causing her to look in the opposite direction. "There is no such thing."

"There is!" She boldly walked up to him now, and looked him in the eye. "My sister, Ruby, found it with her husband and the jeweled dagger proves it."

"Now, that makes no sense at all."

"My mother, bless her soul, bought jeweled daggers from a blind old hag in order to conceive a child."

"So you are a witch, then?" he asked, taking his arm from around the boy's shoulders.

"Nay, I am not," she assured him. "My mother acted only on a superstition."

"A superstition that involved true love?" he asked.

"Yes. She was told that for every dagger purchased she'd have a child – which came true. And if she named the children after the stones in the hilts, that child would someday find true love."

"Ah, so that explains your odd name of Sapphire, and your sister's name of Ruby. Are there more siblings?" He raised a brow. "Perhaps one of you is named Lapis Lazuli?"

"Nay," she said. "But my twin sisters are named Amber and Amethyst."

"And if you had a brother would she have named the poor boy after a gemstone as well?"

"There was no chance of that. You see, when my mother tried to steal a fifth dagger, a curse was placed upon her. She was to have all girls and lose a boy as well as her true love for what she'd done."

"What happened to her?" asked Dugald.

"She died birthing my baby brother, who had one black eye and one of bright orange."

"This whole story seems concocted," growled Roe. "You are making this all up, aren't you?"

"I promise you, 'tis the truth. And if my father had not blamed my mother's death on the daggers and discarded them, I'd have my sapphire dagger today – and my true love. I'd not be married to that deceitful wretch that holds the title of my husband."

"Lady Sapphire, you mustn't say that." Dugald looked up to Roe nervously.

"Don't worry, I won't take my hand to her face the way you did to Erin, bruising her for all to see," said Roe. "I cannot and will not accept this kind of behavior, Dugald. For this, you must be punished."

"I didn't hurt Erin, I assure you, my lord!"

"He wouldn't hurt her," interrupted Sapphire. "And I find it amusing you are so willing to punish a boy when you know not the truth, yet you saw with your own eyes the baron hurt your mother and yet you let him walk away unscathed."

Roe seemed to think for a moment and then turned back to Dugald. "All right. I'll give you the benefit of the doubt this time. But if I find you've been with her again, I'll have to take proper action. You are not to see Erin ever again, not even in secret. Do you understand me?"

"I do, my lord," the boy said sullenly, his shoulders slumping and his head falling forward. "Thank you, my lord."

"Good. Now go find my squire, Waylon, and take my horse from him so he can attend to my other needs. I'll expect to see you working twice as hard now to make up for your mistake."

"Of course, my lord," said Dugald, and he hurried out of the stable.

Roe turned back to Sapphire, but she just shook her head.

"You seem disappointed, Baroness. Please do tell me why."

"Stop calling me Baroness," she told him. "I despise that man and if I could reverse time, I would not be married to him at all. And I find it appalling that you should order a boy to keep away from the girl with whom he has fallen in love."

"I've had an official complaint from the girl's father," Roe explained. "As Lord of Rye, I need to address this issue and find an answer to the problem."

"Then find an answer to my problem, too," she told him. "Kill off that bastard so I no longer have to be his wife."

Two stableboys entered just then, and Roe placed his hand under her elbow and escorted her toward the door.

"Walk with me," he told her. "I'll not have the hired help hearing a noble speak this way, nor will I have tongues wagging within my own walls that the lord was alone in the stable with the baron's wife."

She said nothing to him at all until they got to the garden of the castle. Purple larkspur and red poppies were in full bloom. Coming here always took Sapphire's breath away, as the gardens were so pretty.

"I love flowers," she told him. "These are so colorful."

"They are my mother's favorites as well. She brought them here years ago, as a whole field of them grow outside the castle walls and just over the hill."

"I'd like to see that some day," she said. "It sounds very romantic."

"Get that delusional idea out of your head right now, my little lark. You know as well as I that there is no such thing as romance or true love, especially in a marriage. Two people are married for alliances and having heirs only."

"I don't believe that," she said. "But I know that by being married to the baron, I'll have neither true love nor heirs. He has been sampling every woman in the castle trying to find one who'll be planted with his seed, but to no avail."

"Is that what you were doing at the Bucket of Blood Tavern?" he asked with a raised brow. "Sampling the wares and trying to conceive a child?"

"You swine!" she spat, wrapping her arms around her and turning away. "And to think I let you defile me and even enjoyed it. Now I see what a fool I've been."

"I told you, you'd enjoy it," he answered with a chuckle. "But we both know you were defiled long before I ever laid a hand on you."

"I am not a whore," she told him, sitting down on a stone bench, looking in the opposite direction. "I told you I wasn't to begin with, yet you insisted on pushing yourself on me."

"Pushing?" He sounded amused and sat down next to her. "If I remember correctly, you were begging me to take you."

Just the thought of their night together had her body already responding. But she didn't like the way the man was talking to her, and she had to get away from him before she said something that would anger him. If not, he'd be sending her away, once again, with the baron. She couldn't take the chance.

"Well, you can't blame a woman for wanting to feel the same elation as a man once in awhile."

"So . . . you're saying you do not feel . . . promiscuous while bedding your husband?"

"Why do you even ask me that when it doesn't matter? I

was betrothed to you, yet I was given away when you couldn't even see to send a missive to your worrying mother. I should think you'd feel terrible for the way you've behaved."

"I could say the same about you."

She looked at him and her heart ached. If only he had been here when she'd arrived at the castle, then she wouldn't be in this situation. But now, because of him, she was stuck in a loveless marriage with a man who would never be able to give her children. All her dreams, all her hopes were dashed away, and she had naught to look forward to in this lifetime. It was all because of the handsome man she could not have, who was named Roe Sexton.

"We all make mistakes, my lord. The biggest mistake I ever made was agreeing with my father when he betrothed me to you!"

She walked away quickly, not wanting to hear anything else he had to say. The man of her dreams had just entered her life and it had turned into a nightmare. He thought she was naught more than a whore and wanted nothing to do with her. And the saddest part was, she was starting to feel like one. She realized now that one night of ecstasy was not worth the hell she would have to live through every day, seeing the only man who could make her feel alive, and not being able to even touch him.

She ran to the kitchen hoping to find Lady Katherine, because she needed a mother figure near her in her time of great need.

ROE WATCHED his little lark running through the gardens, the long tippets of her sleeves flowing in the breeze as she crossed the grounds. Her hair fanned out behind her, making her look like an ethereal goddess.

By the rood, he had never expected to see her here right inside his castle walls. And never in a million years had he thought he'd ever be betrothed to a woman as beautiful and as witty as Lady Sapphire. His loins stirred for her still, even more now that he'd seen her in her natural setting. She'd be a perfect wife for any man but, unfortunately, it would never be him.

"Damn," he cursed aloud, wishing he had returned earlier, or even sent a missive to his mother while he'd been away. Sapphire should have been his wife, not the wife of that seething despicable cur, Baron Walter Poussin. He couldn't stand by and do nothing while Sapphire spent the night in that man's bed. It would drive him mad to know that another man was touching her when all he wanted was to wrap her in his arms and never let her go.

Besides, the man beat women. That was something he couldn't tolerate. He needed to do something to break up this farce of a marriage before the girl was hurt further.

"Oh, there you are, my lord," said his squire, Waylon, entering the gardens with Dugald right behind him. Waylon was a tall young man of eight and ten years, nearing his time for knighthood. He had long blond hair pulled back in a queue and a scraggly beard and mustache. He had been a loyal squire, staying with Roe the entire time he campaigned in France. "Did you want me to take the rust off your armor now, milord? Or perhaps polish your sword?"

Roe surveyed Waylon who looked like hell, dirty and smelly from being on the road so long. Then he looked at Dugald with his fresh face and clean hair, depicting an image of being proper instead of bedraggled like his squire. My, how the tables had turned. Roe wondered if he looked as bad as Waylon, or if he smelled as nasty. He also found himself wondering what Sapphire thought of him – the oddest part being that he realized he really cared.

"Egads, you smell, Waylon," he said with a scowl. "You need to clean and shave that hayfield upon your face before you sup at my table."

"My lord?" Waylon picked up an arm and took a sniff. "Do I smell?" he asked Dugald.

"Not any more than Lord Sexton," said the boy, who then looked at him and smiled. Roe had known Dugald since he was a child and couldn't be angry with him when he knew the boy was only jesting with him like they used to do years ago. He was fond of Dugald, and knew in his heart there was no way this boy could ever hurt a woman. He felt bad now that he told him he couldn't see Erin because he really liked the young girl as well.

"Well, you two. Are you going to stand there gawking at me like beached fish, or are you going to do something about the smell in this garden? And I assure you, I don't mean the roses."

"My lord?" asked Waylon.

"Have the servants draw me a bath anon," he commanded. He looked across the garden. "Oh, I see the tub set up in the sun with the water already warming. Tell them I'll require a tent above it for privacy. And find me some soap and a sharp edge because I'm going to find my face again under all this hair."

"Aye, milord, at once," said Waylon. "And I'll also find you a fresh set of clothes to go with it."

They started away, but Roe called out to Dugald.

"Dugald. Come here," he said.

The boy turned around, surprised and ran back to his side.

"Aye, milord, what can I do for you?"

"Tell me the truth. Did you hit Erin?"

The boy's head shook furiously. "Nay, Lord Sexton. I give you my word I never hurt her."

"Then someone else is hitting her and I need to do something to stop it."

"But what?" he asked.

"I'm not sure, but I assure you I'll find the man who is hurting her and put it an end to this myself."

CHAPTER 5

Daughters of the Dagger

Sapphire walked past the garden, heading for the great hall, as the meal was about to be served. She'd helped Lady Katherine in the kitchen and while the woman tried to find out what was bothering her, she'd remained silent.

How could Sapphire tell her she'd gone to bed with her son when she was married to the baron? And how could she be forgiven for the sin that would send her straight to hell? She needed to keep this a secret, and therefore couldn't even take the chance of confessing it to the priest. Not really sure what to do, right now she just wanted to get through the night. And as if it weren't bad enough that she'd have to sit through the meal looking at Lord Sexton, now she'd also have to decide where she planned on sleeping tonight.

As she passed by the gardens, she spied the bath tent and wondered whom it was being prepared for. She loved baths. If the water felt warm enough from the sun, she might just tell her handmaid, Corina, that she'd skip the meal in place of a bath instead.

Curious, she decided to stop inside and test the warmth of the water for herself. Pulling back the flap of the tent, she entered, only to stop in her tracks when she saw Lord Roe Sexton sitting naked in a tub of water. He peered into the back side of a shiny platter, and used the edge of a sharp blade to remove his beard and mustache.

"Oh!" she exclaimed in surprise. He lowered the platter slowly, and rested the knife on the edge of the tub. The wooden barrel being used as a tub was lined with a large, long cloth for comfort against splinters. A small table next to the tub held items such as a soft ball of soap, rose petals, and herbs to sprinkle in the water for scent. A wadded-up piece of cloth he'd been using to wash himself dripped water as it balanced precariously on the edge of the tub, threatening to fall to the ground at any minute.

"Have you come for another romp, my little lark?" he asked. Then he leaned forward, dunking his head and face into the water and came back up with a sharp intake of breath.

"Is the water cold, my lord?" she asked snidely, not liking what he'd insinuated by his remark.

"Not as cold as you think." He got to his feet, exposing his nakedness to her. Without meaning to do it, her eyes fastened on his prominent arousal, verifying his words were true. She turned quickly and held a hand up to her face to block her view.

"Like I said last night, I don't buy the modesty act at all," he grumbled. She heard the sloshing of water as he exited the tub and could feel his presence as he stood directly behind her. "Turn around, Sapphire."

"Nay." She kept her hand hiding her face.

"Look at me." He reached out and gently lowered her hand. Slowly, she turned her head, looking upward to meet with his perusing, bright blue eyes. "I don't want you coupling with that bastard again. Nor do I want him raising a finger to hurt you."

Sapphire could barely concentrate on his words. Since he'd shaved, it revealed the angles of his face and he looked even more handsome than he had with the mustache and beard. She even noticed a dimple in his chin. His long, dark hair dripped water that ran in rivulets down his sturdy chest.

"Why should you care?" she asked, boldly. "After all, you think I am naught more than a . . . a whore." She found that she could barely say the word.

"Hush," he told her, but she kept on talking.

"I was only in the tavern in the first place, trying to get away from my life of doom."

"Please, be quiet."

"But when you dragged me upstairs to suffice your –"

His mouth came down upon hers and, once again, she found herself weakened under his touch. His lips were strong and sensuous, yet at the same time gentle and caring. Then he pulled his mouth away slowly and they gazed into each other's eyes. A slight shiver ran through her as a delightful tingle danced across her skin. And though she felt herself being drawn in, she didn't want to fall prey to his wily ways once again.

". . . manly needs," she finished her sentence.

Before she had a chance to say more, his lips were upon hers again and she found herself falling fast into a whirlwind of sensuous pleasure. Sapphire reached up and grabbed his head, her fingers entangling in his wet hair as she pulled him closer to her. She couldn't stop herself. She wanted him, and his kiss was driving her mad.

Hungrily, she kissed him again, more forceful than she'd intended. His arms closed around her as his hands slipped down her back and he pulled her into him, squeezing her buttocks. The strain of his manhood pushed against her, and also against her own reckless need. Suddenly, she could think of naught else than a repeat of their throes of passion from last night. This needed to stop quickly or, in a matter of minutes, she'd be naked in the tub of water making love to him, with anyone able to walk in and catch them in the act.

Pulling away, she slapped him hard across the face. The sound of skin against skin echoed loudly against his freshly-shaven face. He jerked backward, surprised, and his hand went to his cheek. Roe looked vulnerable in this state and also so alluring, and that only made things worse.

"Was that foreplay?" he asked her with a wry smile that proved he had dimples at the corners of his mouth when his lips turned upward, as well as the dimple on his chin.

"I am a married woman," she reminded him.

"Aye, and you've gone to extremes to point out how much you hate your husband."

"I am also a lady!" Her arms folded across her chest.

"Of course." He ran a hand through his wet hair and let out a sigh. "I'm sorry, Lady Sapphire, I got carried away. I just can't stop thinking about last night." He looked down to his aroused form. "As you can see."

"Then do something about it," she told him.

"I thought that was what I was doing when you slapped me."

"Not that," she said. "I mean, do something about getting me out of my marriage to the baron."

"It isn't that easy, sweetheart. The church is highly against annulments, and very strict about it as well. And as you know, there is no rule against how a man treats his wife or about how many mistresses he takes to his bed."

"And as you know, there *is* a rule saying any man finding his wife has coupled with another man, has the right to see to her punished as he wishes. No one would bat an eye if he decided the punishment to be death."

"You should have thought of that before you ever made love with me, sweetheart."

"I assure you, I never intended for that to happen."

"Well, what did you think would happen when you showed up at a place like the Bucket of Blood Tavern wearing the clothes of a whore, not to mention being unescorted?"

"I didn't know."

"You are naïve, darling, and I think I will have to teach you the ways of the world."

"Roe, the meal is being served," came his mother's voice from outside the curtain. "Is someone in there with you?"

"Now, Mother, why would you think I would take someone to my bath?" he called out.

"Because I thought I heard Sapphire's voice in there. I can also see shadows through that curtain and I see her gown."

Roe turned quickly, his hands covering his groin at her words. Sapphire found herself giggling from his sudden modesty from his own mother.

"Find a way to get me out of this marriage," she whispered. "If you don't, you may have to sentence me to death, because I would kill the man by my own hand before I ever let him touch me again."

She hurried out of the tent to find Roe's mother standing there.

"Lady Katherine, it's not what you think," she said with a forced smile.

"And what is it, my dear, that I would be thinking right now?" Lady Katherine arched an eyebrow as she spoke.

"That I was in there satisfying your son's needs – because I wasn't."

"My body can vouch for that, Mother, so believe her," called out Roe's deep voice from inside the tent.

Lady Katherine looked around quickly, making sure no one was watching, and then she put her arm around Sapphire and whispered into her ear.

"I wish you had married my son instead of the baron. I would love for you to be my daughter by marriage and bear many grandchildren for me."

ROE PARTED the curtains of the tent and watched as his mother walked away with her arm around Sapphire. He had heard every word she'd said.

"I wish that as well, Mother," he said softly, his heart aching as he watched them head toward the castle. "I wish that as well."

CHAPTER 6

S apphire sat at the dais for the midday meal with Roe at the middle of the trestle table on one side of her, and the priest from the village, Father Geoffrey, on her other side. Had her husband not been away on business in town, he would have been sitting next to her instead. She was grateful for his absence.

Roe's mother sat at his left side and his uncle, next to her. Because of the way they were seated, Sapphire had to share a cup and trencher with Roe. She was secretly happy for this and only hoped she'd be able to concentrate during the meal.

"My lady, would you care for some spiced wine?" Roe held the goblet out to her. When she reached for it, his hand brushed against hers briefly before he pulled it away. A wave of excitement rushed through her from his mere touch, and she lowered her gaze to the table instead of looking directly at him. After taking a sip, she handed it back to him. His fingers stretched out and rubbed against the top of her left hand as he took it from her.

Sapphire's eyes shot upward by his action. Their gazes

interlocked – desire as well as intimacy passing briefly between them.

"He didn't even give you a ring?" he asked under his breath.

"No time, I suppose, as the wedding was very rushed," she answered, subconsciously covering her left hand.

She surveyed the tray of food the servant laid upon the table. The carver stepped forward with a sharp knife in his hand and nodded first toward Lord Sexton and then to her.

"If I may carve the meat, my lord and lady?" The carver stood with a large platter holding lamb roasted with vinegar and salt. Sapphire enjoyed lamb on occasion, but her favorite was the Doucettes – a pork and egg pie seasoned with pepper and sweetened with honey.

"Aye," said Roe, and she felt as if the servant had addressed them as a married couple. Almost as if she were the lady of the household, even though his mother took that position since Roe was not married. She liked the feeling and wished it were true.

The carver sliced the roasted meat in front of them and placed some on the trencher, an old stale crust of bread used to hold the food, which lay between them.

"That'll be all, thank you," said Roe with a nod. The man headed down the table to carve for Roe's mother and uncle as well.

Roe spoke as he dished out peas and root vegetables and added them to the trencher along with a piece of Sapphire's favorite pie.

"I would have given you a ring worth talking about," muttered Roe under his breath. The priest overheard him and joined in the conversation.

"Lady Sapphire, how are you enjoying married life to the baron?" asked the priest. "After all, you have married someone of a higher rank than just a lord, and should be very happy at the results of your betrothal."

"Actually," said Sapphire, clearing her throat. "My father betrothed me to Lord Roe Sexton. But Roe's uncle thought him dead and carelessly married me off to the baron instead."

"Is this true?" The priest looked over at Roe.

"It is, I'm afraid," Roe answered. "But had I known I'd been betrothed," his hooded eyes perused Sapphire, drinking her in, making her feel a bit uncomfortable with the priest so near, "then I would have hurried home and it would have been my wedding instead."

"What a shame, what a shame," said the priest, shaking his head.

"Would that be grounds for an annulment?" asked Roe. Sapphire could hear the hope in his voice.

"Well, I believe it could. However, since Lady Sapphire agreed to the marriage, the request might not be granted by the pope."

"Well, what would be considered worthy of being granted an annulment?" asked Sapphire.

"If one of the two in question was already married, I suppose," explained the priest. "Or if the woman could not bear the man an heir."

"Really?" asked Sapphire with newfound hope. "Then I want an annulment, as I have not been able to give my husband an heir. He has stopped sleeping with me because of it."

"Oh my!" The priest blessed himself and said a whispered prayer.

"What do we do?" Roe asked Father Geoffrey.

"Well, Lady Sapphire's husband would have to be the one to request the annulment, posing his complaint about her being barren."

"He'd never do that, I am sure." Sapphire took a bite of food and looked down to her trencher. Things seemed to be going from bad to worse.

"I would like to drink to my son," announced Lady Katherine, holding her goblet high. "Who will join me in celebrating the return of my missing son?"

"Mother, please," grumbled Roe. "I was not missing."

"Aye," agreed his uncle, standing and raising his goblet. "To Lord Roe Sexton, may he someday be as happy as the baron and his wife, Lady Sapphire."

Shouts and cheers were heard and the minstrels up in the gallery started playing music. Ethereal notes from the rote, five-stringed harp, floated down into the great hall joined in by the sound of a frestelle, a flute that resembled a panpipe. Rhythm was kept by a minstrel tapping lightly on the naker, a double drum. And the tinkling of clochetes, or small bells, rounded out the delightful tune.

"I wouldn't wish that on you," Sapphire whispered to Roe, raising the goblet and pretending to drink to his toast as well.

Dessert included spiced pears cooked in wine, and blackberry pie that Roe had said was his favorite and he'd eaten most of it himself. The servants cleared away the trenchers, collecting them to be given to the beggars outside the castle gates, or to the hounds. The trestle tables were then taken apart with half a dozen men working to move the heavy boards from the trestles that held them in place. And once the area was cleared, the room was ready for entertainment.

"Let us all dance," said Lady Katherine, rising from the dais and heading toward the stairs. She stopped just behind Roe's padded chair – a chair that designated him as lord of the castle. "I would expect you'd be dancing with Lady Sapphire since her husband is away on business," she told her son.

"Mother, I am not sure that is a good idea," protested Roe.

"I don't need to dance," said Sapphire, smiling slightly and looking out to the floor at the happy lords and ladies who found pleasure in their spouse's presence. This saddened her, since she had always loved to dance. She'd even taught the steps to her sisters while growing up, and forced her father to dance with each of them in turn after the meals at Blackpool Castle. Releasing a deep sigh, she realized she would never dance again. That is, because she would refuse to dance with the baron, and no man would have the courage to stand in his place.

"You do need to dance," said Roe, standing and pulling out her chair. "You will dance with me, my lady. I'll not let you sit there so sullenly without participating in the merriment."

She planned on protesting, but he didn't seem to want to take no for an answer. Besides, she secretly wanted to dance with him, and now that her husband was gone, 'twas a perfect opportunity.

He helped her from her chair and held out his arm. Hesitantly, she placed her hand atop his arm, being guided from the dais to the main floor. The music started up a lively tune and he bowed to her gallantly. She, in return, curtsied. Then he took her arm and they moved forward. He spun her around next, turning her in a full circle.

"You look beautiful tonight, Lady Sapphire."

Her eyes met his and she drank in the beauty of his

freshly-shaven face. She wanted nothing more than to run her hands over it, but she couldn't touch it.

"Thank you," she said with a slight nod, turning to dance with her corner who happened to be Roe's uncle.

"You seem to like dancing with Roe," said Roe's uncle, Lord Henry. "However, I don't think your husband would take kindly to your unruly behavior."

"Unruly behavior?" she asked. "I assure you, my lord, my interest is in the dance only."

She turned back to Roe. He reached out and touched her at her waist lightly as he guided her across the floor. He was so handsome and she felt the attraction between them immediately. Her stomach flipped inside at the mere thought of being in his embrace once again.

"Where will you be sleeping tonight, my lady?" he asked softly.

"Anywhere but with the baron," she whispered back, and turned once more to greet her corner. Unfortunately, this time instead of Lord Henry, she reeled backward when she realized Baron Walter Poussin was standing there with his arm outstretched, waiting for her.

"Lord husband," she gasped. "I thought you were going to be in town until nightfall."

"I can see that," he said, grabbing her roughly, shooting a daggered look at Roe. "I have also heard from the priest just now that you and Roe have been asking questions about an annulment."

When she didn't answer, he gripped her by the wrist tightly. "I warn you to drop the request, because I will never agree to it. And should Roe Sexton get involved, I will stir up trouble for him like you could never imagine."

She turned back to Roe, but stepped away from him when he went to take her by the arm.

"I don't think I want to dance anymore," she told him.

He looked bewildered, but then noticed the baron standing behind her, and his smile turned into a frown. "I can see why. Don't let him stop you from enjoying yourself," he said, once more reaching out for her.

She stepped away and shook her head, and ran to the corner of the room. Lady Katherine noticed and followed.

"What is it, my dear?" she asked, putting her arm around Sapphire.

"I feel so trapped," Sapphire relayed. "I no longer wish to dance with my husband nor your son, and yet I have nowhere to go to be alone."

Roe walked over to join them. He gave his mother a glance that said he wanted to be alone with her, and his mother quickly walked away.

"Sapphire, I heard what you said and you are wrong. You do have somewhere to go." He glanced toward the baron with a scowl upon his face, and then back at her. "I will give you my chamber as your own and I will sleep in the great hall instead. This should ensure your safety."

"Thank you," she said, "but I fear my husband will not like that."

"Then I will post a guard at the door if I have to, but you will not be going back with that man if I have anything to say about it."

"But he is my husband," she reminded him.

"He's also my enemy now, since he has hurt you as well as my mother. If he so much as tries to fight my decision, I will bring him to trial for having raised a hand to my mother."

Sapphire noticed her handmaid, Corina, waiting at the entranceway of the great hall. The handmaiden had been assigned to her when she'd first come to the castle, but Sapphire could see lately that something was troubling the short, plump girl.

"I'll go now to your solar then," she said, brushing past her husband without acknowledging him, collecting up her handmaid and rushing down the hall.

"Sir George," Roe called out, bringing the knight to his side.

"Aye, milord?" The man stood next to him at attention.

"Stand guard over Lady Sapphire outside my solar door tonight and do not let her husband enter."

"Turn away her own husband?" the man asked in question.

"You heard my orders, now go."

"Aye, my lord," the man said with a confused look upon his face, hurrying away.

"Roe, what was that all about?" asked Lady Katherine in question, walking up, having overheard part of his conversation.

"I gave Sapphire my solar, Mother, and placed a guard at the door. I will not let the baron hurt her again."

"You have no right to do that," she reminded him. "He is her husband."

"By right, I should have been her husband. The negotiations were made for me, Mother. And since I am not dead, I will have her as my wife, after all."

"Roe, as much as I want you to be married to Sapphire, 'tis too late. Just release the idea."

"She spoke of finding true love," he told his mother. "She also said she'd never find it with her husband."

"So you think you can help her find it?"

"I don't know," he said, shaking his head slightly. "But I do know even with no love between us, she would still be better off with me than the baron. I would never raise a hand to harm her."

"You sound as if you care for her, Son." His mother placed her hand on his arm.

"I do. And tell me, Mother, do you really care for your husband, Lord Henry? Because there is something about my uncle I have never liked."

"I married him at the death of your father to secure our holdings in the family name," she explained.

"But part of it was already yours upon inheritance."

"Only a third, Son. I didn't want to lose the rest that your father worked so hard to keep. But now that you have returned, it doesn't matter. You are his heir, so everything belongs to you now. I know you will protect the castle, the lands, and the people of Rye as well."

"I will, Mother, I assure you that."

Just then, several of the dockmen rushed in, conversing quickly with the guards. Curious to know what had them so upset, Roe headed in their direction. His uncle and the baron followed.

"Godfrey," said Roe, greeting his old friend. "What is it that has you so upset?"

"My lords," he said, bowing his head to all three of them. The men with him did the same but stayed silent. "There is trouble and deceit, Lord Sexton, and I don't know what to think of it."

"How so?" asked Henry.

"Aye, how so?" mimicked the baron.

"The merchants are complaining, my lords, as well as the sheepherders. They say that fifty tuns of wool has gone missing."

"Missing?" asked Roe. "What do you mean?"

"The sheepherders of Dungeness have approached the merchants personally, saying they need their pay for the goods delivered to them. However, the merchants say they have never received the wool. This is the second time a shipment has been lost in the past four months, my lord."

"I'm sure they've just handled their ledgers poorly," said Henry.

"Aye," added the baron. "I have overseen the Romney Marshes personally, as Castle Lydd is not far from there and those are my lands. Actually, the sheepherders are always falling asleep while part of their flocks wander off. They are careless and have probably just misplaced the wool."

"Misplaced fifty tuns of wool?" asked Roe. "Nay, this sounds suspicious to me."

"There's plenty wool in all of England," said Henry. "Since the plague and the lack of people, the task of sheepherding, which requires only a scant number of workers, has increased and it infiltrates the land."

"Perhaps too much," agreed Roe. "And with the king's new taxes and trying to control the price by strengthening the demand for our fine wool overseas, it opens the door to smuggling."

"Smuggling?" asked Godfrey. "Do you really think so, my lord?"

"I do. Have you seen any suspicious ships leaving port lately?" Roe asked.

"They've all been accounted for, my lord."

"Has the dockmaster been collecting the taxes from the ships that come and go, transporting goods across the channel?"

"I believe so, my lord."

"Then there must be someone we're overlooking. Someone everyone trusts who is pulling the wool over everyone's eyes so to speak."

"Sexton, enough with your feeble humor," said the baron. "This is preposterous! There is no way smugglers could get fifty tuns through the streets without anyone seeing them being moved."

"Unless they're smuggling it with the help of some of the merchants. Perhaps secret tunnels or passageways beneath some of the buildings in town," explained Roe.

"That's ridiculous," said Henry.

"It's not out of the question," said Roe with a shake of his head.

"I'll look into this matter myself," said Baron Lydd. "After all, it is from my lands that the wool is disappearing. I'll go to the marshes of Dungeness on the morrow and see how the sheepherders are faring."

"I'll come with you," said Roe, evoking a distinct reaction from the baron.

"Nay," said the baron. "I am capable of handling it, Sexton. I want you nowhere near my lands."

Roe had never meant to go with him, but wanted to see if the man would react, which he did. This told him that something was amiss, and the baron was most likely involved.

"Fine," said Roe. "And I have reconsidered and want you off my land after all, so don't bother coming back."

"So be it," snapped the baron. "Then I'll just collect my wife and, tomorrow, we'll be on our way."

He stepped forward, but Roe pulled his sword and held it in front of the man.

"Egads, Roe, what are you doing?" shouted Henry. "You are acting like the man is our enemy when he is our ally."

"You'll not take Sapphire anywhere," he warned him. "She no longer wishes to be near you."

"I'm married to her, Sexton," snarled the baron. "Or have you forgotten?"

"I haven't forgotten the tales she tells me of how you've beaten her and also taken every woman you could to your bed. That doesn't sound like marriage to me. That sounds like a man so desperate that he'd do anything to get what he wanted. What is it you want, Lydd? And Uncle," he said, nodding toward Henry, "why were you so fast to say I was dead and hand over my betrothed without sending a messenger over the channel to find out? It seems to me, you never even discussed the new marriage with Earl Blackpool, Sapphire's father."

"There was no need," said Henry. "We had the dowry and the girl, so why make waves by sending her back? Besides, we couldn't send a man overseas and risk his life."

"We?" asked Roe. "So, are you saying that you have acquired part of Sapphire's dowry as well?"

"'Twas an agreement I had with the baron," he admitted.

"An agreement that seems odd to me. Odd that you, Baron Lydd, would allow someone to take half of what you felt was rightfully yours."

"What are you saying, Sexton?" the baron ground out. "Just spit it out already and stop with your feeble games."

Roe slowly replaced his sword at his side. "What all did the dowry include?" He needed to know. Neither of the men said anything. "I will send a missive to Blackpool tomorrow and schedule a meeting with the earl to discuss what has transpired here."

"Stop it, Sexton," said the baron, sounding defeated. "If you want the girl, take her, but I am not returning any of the dowry."

"So noble of you to offer me something that was mine all along. But tell me, how do you propose we get the marriage annulled? And why are you so willing to give her up when, a moment ago, you told me I couldn't have her?"

"Let's discuss this in the morning," said Henry, placing his hand on Roe's shoulder.

"Nay!" Roe pushed it off. He then looked over at the dockmen. "Keep a close eye on every ship and every sailor and every piece of cargo upon it that comes or goes from the port of Rye. I will be contacting the Baron of the Cinque Ports and will discuss this matter with him immediately."

"He is gone and will not return for several weeks," said Godfrey. "And he is joined by many of the portsmen and crews of the ships that protect the channel. They have started on their journey to Yarmouth for the annual herring festival," he told Roe.

"Damn, that's right," said Roe. "Then I'll have to wait, but tell the dockmen, merchants and the sheepherders, too, that I'll be looking into this personally and hopefully have answers for them soon."

"Aye, milord, thank you, milord." The men bowed and Roe

dismissed them with a wave of his hand and they hurried away.

"You've not heard the last of me," snarled the baron, storming across the great hall.

"Roe, the baron will look into the matter. And the baron of the Cinque Ports is in charge of the ports, not you. Just let them investigate, and don't get involved," warned Henry.

"If I wait, it may be too late," he told him. "And I have a feeling I know just the place to start looking."

CHAPTER 7

Daughters of the Dagger

Sapphire awoke early, having had the best night's sleep in a long time. She turned over in Roe's bed and stretched her arms lazily above her head.

"Good morning, my lady," said her handmaiden, who had slept on the pallet at the foot of her bed. "'Tis a beautiful morning, and the sun is shining. Just look," she said, pulling open the wooden shutters over the window that blocked out the night air. The sun streamed in and caught Sapphire by surprise. She squinted and blocked her eyes with her hand.

"It is so bright, Corina. Can't you turn down the sun?"

The handmaid laughed and so did Sapphire. Then the girl flipped back the coverlet, all but pulling Sapphire from the bed.

"You seem to be in a hurry this morning, Corina."

"I just enjoy the morning. Now let's get you up and dressed, my lady." She took Sapphire by the arm and pulled her over to the washbasin. "Perhaps you'd like to wash your face while I ready your gown?"

Sapphire stopped and crossed her arms over her chest, looking at the girl. Sapphire had slept in her shift since most of her clothes were still in the chamber with the baron and there was no way she wanted to enter his room last night to get them.

"Corina, where is it you need to be?"

"My lady?" Corina picked up Sapphire's blue velvet gown and held it to her chest. "Why do you think I need to be somewhere?"

"Because you have been my handmaid for four months now and never once have you rushed me into dressing. Actually, if you have forgotten, I am the one who usually rises before you and has to rouse you from your slumber."

"Oh, I am sorry, my lady, but I have lied to you." The girl looked frightened and tightened her grip on Sapphire's gown. Sapphire reached over and gently took it from her.

"If you clench this any tighter, you'll crush it," she told the maid. "And it truly is one of my favorite gowns, given to me by my father. Now sit down, Corina, and tell me what troubles you." She guided the girl to the bed and made her sit upon it.

"I am frightened, my lady."

"Of what?" she asked. "Has the baron been trying to get you into his bed as well? You can tell me, Corina. I truly will not hold it against you, even if you have laid with him."

"Nay, my lady. I would never. But I do have a young man back in my homeland of Dungeness who I have not seen in months now."

"And you're frightened of him?"

"Nay, I am excited. You see, while we plan on marrying someday, he works sheering the sheep that graze in the marshlands. And I . . ." she held her hand to her stomach . . . "I have some news to tell him."

"Corina?" Sapphire's smile spread across her face. "Are you by any chance with child?"

The girl looked up sharply, her gaze unsettled.

"If you are, I think it is the most wonderful news," she added to ease the girl's mind.

Corina let out a sigh of relief. "I am," she admitted, smiling and laughing and crying all in the same breath. "I am with child and today I felt the baby move."

"How exciting!" Sapphire sat next to the girl and hugged her. "Then you must go to the man you love anon and tell him you are to have a child together."

"But I must take care of you, my lady."

"Nonsense." Sapphire walked over to the table and picked up her pouch. She slipped a gold coin from within and handed it to the girl. "Take this to your lover, and stay with him until the baby is born."

"But – what about my position as your handmaid?"

"You can return whenever you want, and I will not turn you away. I will find another handmaid to take your place for now. Corina, having children is the most important thing in life. That and true love, which I see in your eyes for this man. 'Tis clear to me that you and your lover hold a deep love for each other. Now go! And take with you my blessings for a healthy child."

"Are you sure, my lady?"

"I am."

"Oh, thank you," she said, jumping up and giving Sapphire another hug. "I knew you would understand." In a second, Corina had left and closed the door behind her.

Sapphire dressed quickly, thinking of how happy she was for the girl. She wished it were her running off pregnant to tell her lover the good news. She didn't know what the day would bring, nor if the baron would be angry that she'd spent the night in Roe's chamber. Whatever happened, she was sure Roe would protect her, and that was something she truly admired about the man.

As she quickly ran a brush over her hair, she decided to wear it long, although a married woman always wore it up. She didn't feel like a married woman, so it mattered not to her. She secured her pouch at her side, feeling the last of the coins her father had given her within it.

It was a very generous act to give an entire gold piece to her handmaid, but it would be enough for her and her lover to live on until the baby was born. And when Corina returned – if Sapphire was still at Castle Rye, she would see to it that the girl was given back her position as handmaid, as well as have a position for her husband, too. She would also lend a hand personally in taking care of their baby.

She pulled open the door, taken aback for a moment. She'd forgotten Roe had placed a guard in the corridor.

"Good morning," she said with a nod and hurried down the hall and out to the courtyard. The breeze blew against her face and the sun shone brightly. The emptiness inside her chipped away just by the mere thought that Corina would be returning with her baby soon.

She felt like riding today, and headed for the stable to talk to Dugald. But just before she entered, Dugald ran out and pulled her to the side. Right behind him, a horse shot out like an arrow from a bow. Atop it rode the baron. He pulled back the reins and stopped momentarily, looking down at her with eyes of fire. She expected him to reprimand her, and her body already tensed as the thought crossed her mind that he might hit her.

"Go to him, you little bitch," he said. "But don't think this is the last of it. Remember, you are still married to me!" With that, he turned and sped across the courtyard and over the bridge, leaving the castle – thankfully without her.

"What was that all about?" she asked Dugald.

"Lord Sexton told him to leave, and he also told him he wasn't going to be taking you along with him. He said he wanted you, my lady. I heard it from his own mouth."

"Lord Sexton? Do you mean Roe?" she asked, just to be sure he wasn't somehow speaking of Lord Henry.

"Aye, he did."

Her heart skipped a beat, and she wondered if mayhap things could be different in her life after all. "Where is Roe now?" she asked him.

"Lord Sexton is preparing to leave for town as we speak. I've just saddled his horse, and his squire is preparing to go with him."

"To town?" she asked. "Whatever for?"

Castle Rye was efficient in having everything one needed. Within the castle walls as well as on his demesne, Roe had an alehouse, a church, a stable, his personal blacksmith, and even a mill. Merchants came to sell their wares inside the castle walls nearly every day. He had jugglers and minstrels and mummers for entertainment. The ladies of the castle sewed and spun and weaved. The lord and his men hunted the meat and the villeins and serfs in the village sowed and harvested the crops.

There were cooks to prepare the meals and a steward to

handle the lord's estate and ledgers. The woodward watched his forests for poachers and the kennelgrooms and falconers took care of many of the animals. There was even a wetnurse to feed the babies and an ewerer to help one wash their hands. There was no reason, as far as she could see, to ever need to leave the castle or go to town.

"I heard something about smuggling and I think he is going to town to see what he can find out," Dugald relayed the information.

"Smuggling? That's something I hadn't even considered." She wasn't even concerned about that this morning, as she was feeling lighthearted and carefree now that the baron had left the premises.

"I was hoping to see you down here this morning," the boy told her. "I've saddled a horse for you as well, my lady."

"Oh, wonderful. I do think I'll go for a ride in the field after I break the fast."

Dugald looked back into the stable and Sapphire glanced past him to see Roe as well as his freshly-shaven squire, Waylon, mounting their horses and preparing to leave.

"Go with them, my lady."

She looked up and considered the thought, but realized if Roe were concerned with smugglers, he would not want her tagging along, nor was it appropriate.

"I think I'd rather ride in the fields than to go down to the docks. I like the peacefulness and want to find that patch of red poppies that Lady Katherine loves. Perhaps I'll ask her to go along for a ride as well."

She saw Roe and his squire heading out of the stable. Dugald turned back to her and she noticed the frantic look in his eyes.

"I heard them say they're stopping at the Bucket of Blood Tavern while they're there."

"The Bucket of Blood?" she asked. "Well, then I surely don't want to go! I think I've had my fill of that place the last time I was there with you."

"Erin will be there, my lady. And she'll be wondering why I haven't come back to see her since . . . since . . ."

"Oh," she said with a big nod of her head. "Say no more, Dugald. I'll go along with them and tell her why you haven't come to see her."

"Tell her – I love her," he blurted out. Sapphire just looked at him and shook her head.

"I think that is something you need to tell her yourself. Now how would it look coming from a second party? Really, Dugald, it would mean more if she heard it from your lips, not mine."

"But I'm not allowed to see her again, so how can I tell her? If I go to the inn, Lord Sexton will not trust me and probably think I hit her, which I never would."

"I understand," she said. "I'll take care of things, don't you worry. Now, go fetch my horse so I can follow Lord Sexton and his squire."

"I'll tell them you are going with them, my lady," Dugald suggested.

"Nay," she said, stepping back into a shadow as they exited the stable without seeing her. "I will follow instead, because I have a feeling that the Bucket of Blood Tavern is the last place Lord Sexton would want me to go."

CHAPTER 8

*S*apphire rode through the gates of Castle Rye and over the bridge, able to see Roe and his squire up ahead of her but in the distance. She was mounted in a lady's saddle. Although she was an experienced rider, she could not hold a candle to the speed her sister, Ruby, had while riding a horse, no matter what type of saddle. Ruby could outride any man, any day. Sapphire would be happy with just being able to keep up with the men.

They slowed down when they neared the docks and she was finally able to catch them. They were off their horses and speaking with the dockmaster when she rode up, stopping right behind them.

"Lady Sapphire?" asked Waylon, being the first to notice her.

Roe turned so quickly at hearing her name that she thought he was going to kink his neck. "Sapphire?" he growled. "What the hell are you doing here?" He looked around, noticing she had come alone. "And without an escort

I might add? I thought you learned your lesson last time you indulged in that little escapade."

"You've been here before without an escort?" asked Waylon in surprise.

Roe didn't give her a chance to answer. He tossed the reins to his squire and hurried over to her.

"What's going on?" he asked in a low voice. "Why aren't you back at the castle?"

"I heard you were coming to town and I wanted to go for a ride, so I followed you."

"You followed?" he said loudly, then looked back toward Waylon who just nodded and smiled. Once more, he addressed her. "Why would you do such a thing? And why didn't you make your presence known earlier?"

"I couldn't keep up, my lord, or I would have shouted out."

"Somehow I have trouble believing that," he answered. "Now, are you going to tell me why you're really here or am I going to have to drag it out of you?"

She really didn't want to get Dugald in trouble by telling Roe the true reason she'd followed. But she figured if she remained silent he might do something just to shock her, like reaching up and kissing her to catch her by surprise just to get the answers he needed. She really couldn't have that. After all, she was not covered by her mantle this time, and all eyes on the dock were already upon them. It wasn't every day a lady in one of her best gowns decided to grace the dock rats with her presence.

"Oh, all right, I'll tell you. Dugald heard you were stopping by the Bucket of Blood Tavern and asked me to come along."

"This has something to do with Erin, doesn't it?"

"He wants me to give her a message since you've forbidden him to see her."

"I can imagine," he said. "Probably the coordinates of a secret meeting place."

"Nay," she answered. "He is not that romantic. But he does want me to tell her that he loves her."

"What?" asked Roe. "That boy has a lot to learn. You are not really going to tell her that, and in front of her father, are you? Auley O'Conner hates Dugald. He thinks the boy hit his daughter."

"That's nonsense," said Sapphire. "Someone who gives a message that he loves a girl would never be the same one to hit her."

"I know that," said Roe. "But there is naught you can do to convince the girl's father. Now, promise me that you will not give Erin that message."

"I wasn't planning on it," she said.

"Good. Then there is no need for you to even go inside. After the last time, I don't fancy you anywhere near this tavern." He surveyed her from head to foot, causing the heat to settle in her cheeks. His eyes were piercing as he perused her attire. "At least you're not wearing a scarlet gown this time."

She laughed. "That's a mistake I'll never make again, my lord."

"Come on," Roe told Waylon, mounting his horse. "You stay outside the tavern with Lady Sapphire while I go in and see what I can find out."

Sapphire followed them to the Bucket of Blood Tavern without saying a word. Noticing the squire yawning, she decided to use it to her advantage, as she'd be able to move faster than him. And there was no way in hell she planned on following Roe's orders. There was a lovesick boy back at the stable who was counting on her, and she had an idea how she could bring the two together once again, without Dugald having to disobey Roe.

* * *

ROE HADN'T BEEN INSIDE LONG QUESTIONING the patrons trying to find out anything he could about the missing tuns of wool, when the door opened and he heard shouts and whistles from the men who were drinking and gambling. He knew without turning around that his little lark hadn't obeyed him.

Turning, he saw Sapphire gliding across the room with her bright blue gown sweeping across the dirty rushes of the floor. Waylon ran in right behind her.

"I'm sorry, my lord," shouted his squire. "She rushed in when I was looking the other way." Roe might have believed that if Waylon hadn't ended his sentence with a yawn.

"Don't you mean while you were sleeping?" he asked. "Egads, Waylon, it was but a simple task."

"Not really, my lord, as she has a mind of her own."

"Aye," he agreed, "that is true. I have to admit that nothing about Sapphire is simple."

Sapphire crossed the floor and stopped right next to him. One man called out to her, but it all ended quickly when Roe looked up sharply and rested his hand atop his sword.

"Well, my little lark," he said so only she could hear him. "It seems to me you can't stay away from this place. Did you want me to see if our room is free?"

"Stop it," she said in a whisper. "You know I want naught

of the sort so don't even jest with me. I am here only for Dugald."

"Did I hear you say Dugald?" Erin stood at Roe's elbow. Although the bruise on her face was lightening, he thought he noticed a new scratch on her arm.

"Erin, I'd like you to meet my . . . Lady Sapphire," he said, almost calling her his wife for some odd reason. Mayhap, because to him, they seemed more like a couple than she and the baron. "Sapphire, this is Erin." Roe reached out and mussed the girl's hair the way he always used to when she was young.

Erin scowled at him and straightened her hair with her hand.

"Where's Dugald?" she asked excitedly. Then realizing her father was walking up behind her, she hurriedly scooted off to clean a table.

"Lord Sexton, this is a surprise," said the innkeeper, Auley, stopping to look at Sapphire.

"Auley, I'd like you to meet Lady Sapphire," Roe introduced them.

"Oh, so ye're the baron's wife," he said with a smile and a nod of approval.

"You know the baron?" asked Roe, which seemed to trigger a surprised reaction from Auley.

"I met him . . . once. When he stopped in with yer uncle for a drink. Where are they today?" he asked, looking around.

"Not here," said Roe.

"The baron left his wife with ye?" he asked curiously.

Roe noticed Sapphire opening her mouth to say something and he knew he had to stop her. After all, he didn't want her telling Auley anything. The man was a busybody. Roe knew all about everyone who was a patron at the place as well as the whores who worked the place. Not that he wanted or needed to know but because, through the years, the man just couldn't keep his mouth shut. The alewives went to him for their gossip.

"They're both attending to business," he said. "Lady Sapphire is here at my request. I thought Erin might enjoy meeting her."

"Oh," he said, looking back at his daughter wiping off a table. "I see."

"There is more I'd like to talk to you about," said Roe. "It seems we might have smugglers in Rye."

"Smugglers?" the man asked. "Why would ye say that?"

"Excuse me, my lord, but I'll just talk with Erin while you two conduct your business." Sapphire hurried across the room.

Roe wanted to reach out and grab her and tell her not to go anywhere nor say anything to anyone but, instead, he just nodded. God's eyes, why didn't he turn around right now and take her back to the castle instead of letting her stay here? This could only end poorly. Of that, he was sure.

"I haven't noticed any smugglers," said Auley. "What is missing?"

"A lot of wool," he answered.

"Really, Lord Sexton? I'd think if fifty tuns of wool was being brought through the streets, I woulda seen it, don't ye?"

"How did you know how much was missing?" asked Roe. "I never said the amount."

The man looked suddenly nervous. Roe felt confused. Could Auley have something to do with this? He thought he knew the man. Roe's absence for the last year was proving that everyone had changed while he was gone. He really didn't know anyone anymore.

"I heard it," the man said.

"From who?" asked Roe.

The door to the tavern opened and Roe noticed a couple of sheepherders walk in. One was a woman. The same couple of dockmen who'd come to the castle the other night entered as well.

"From them," Auley said, pointing to the men.

"I see," he answered, realizing it could be true. The dockmen had probably been going to all the merchants and asking questions.

"Father?" Erin walked up with Sapphire at her side. Roe already didn't like the smile plastered across his little lark's face. He wondered just what message from Dugald she'd relayed to the girl after all.

"What do ye want, Erin?" the innkeeper asked.

"Lady Sapphire has asked me to come to the castle to be her lady-in-waiting," replied Erin.

"She did what?" blurted out Roe, not believing what he'd just heard. "Lady Sapphire already has a handmaiden," he told the girl. "So I'm sorry, Erin, but you won't be needed."

The girl looked forlorn, making him feel bad, but there was no way he could have Erin at the castle with Dugald there. Besides, Auley wouldn't like it.

"I released Corina from her position just this morning," Sapphire announced.

"Why would you do a thing like that?" Roe could see Sapphire's plan clearly now.

"She was pregnant and I sent her back to her sheepherder

until after the baby is born. I do need a handmaiden and I think Erin would do nicely."

"Please, Father, can I go?" asked Erin.

"To live at the castle with that stableboy so near ye? Never," the man spat.

"She has paid well, and said there is much more of this, Father." Erin held out her hand filled with coins. Roe could see a few of them were gold.

"Sapphire, what are you doing by giving her all those coins?" asked Roe. "That's not nearly the correct pay for a servant."

"Oh, well, I have more," she said, digging through her pouch.

He reached out and grabbed her wrist and she looked up to him with those innocent eyes and smiled.

"I'm not buying it," he whispered, letting her know that he knew exactly what she was doing.

"Let me see that," said Auley, taking the coins from his daughter's hand. "There's more of this if she comes to the castle to be yer handmaiden?" he asked.

"Much more," Sapphire answered, almost causing Roe to choke. He coughed, trying to give her the message, but she wasn't going to back down until she had what she came for – and that was Erin.

"Put your coins away," Roe told her, noticing the patrons starting to look over at them. "We don't need a melee on our hands, darling. That's more money than some of these people see in a lifetime."

"Of course," she said, drawing the strings tight on her pouch. "So. what is your decision, Mr. O'Conner? Can Erin come to work for me? I assure you she will be taken care of as if she were my own daughter. She will be under the protection of Lord Sexton as well."

"Well," the man said, looking up with squinted eyes and then clasping his fist tightly over the coins. "I suppose so," he said. "But I don't want to find out that stableboy is abusing her."

"You know I wouldn't let anything happen to little Erin," Roe said, wondering what the hell just happened that he was suddenly agreeing to this absurd idea.

"Lord Sexton, I'm not little anymore," Erin reminded him.

He thought about it and nodded. Aye, she was all grown up and he was having a hard time getting used to the fact.

"You realize I'll have to hire someone to take her place at the inn," said Auley.

Before he could stop her, Sapphire reached out and dropped a few more coins into the man's hand. "This should help with that," she told him.

"Sapphire," Roe ground out. "Stop it."

"This will pay for a new hire for the next month," she told the innkeeper.

"And if we stay here any longer, you'll be buying the place next," Roe growled.

"It's settled then. I agree to let her go with ye," said Auley, giving his daughter a quick hug. "Go pack a few things, Erin, and be on yer way."

"Oh, thank you, Father," she said excitedly. "You won't regret this." Erin ran from the room. Her blond hair drawn up into a tail bobbed up and down behind her.

"I already do," her father mumbled, heading back to the drink board.

"So do I," Roe echoed his concern.

"Lord Sexton, did you want to speak with the sheep-herders who just came into the tavern?" asked Waylon. "They might be from Dungeness and know something about the missing wool."

SAPPHIRE FOLLOWED the men to the table, feeling happy with the outcome of things. Dugald was going to be so thankful when he found out Erin was coming to live at the castle. It brought a sense of satisfaction to her that she'd not only helped one woman today, but now she'd helped two. And both of them had desired to spend time with the men they loved. It was just as it should be, and all because of her.

Glancing around the room, she noticed the dark wood shelves and nooks and crannies. The tavern had two large fireplaces, but only one of them was lit. Now that she thought about it, she'd never seen the second fireplace lit in all the months she'd been coming in here, even when some of the nights had been quite chilly. Odd, but she was sure there was a good reason for it. Perhaps Auley couldn't afford to burn both hearths at once.

She wasn't paying much attention to the people at the table that Roe was questioning, but her ears perked up when she heard the woman of the group mention the baron.

"I hear that Baron Lydd has been staying at your castle in Rye," said the woman.

"Aye," answered Roe. "Are you from Lydd?"

"I live there," she said. "We all do." The woman pointed to the two sheepherders with her. "Well, actually, they live on the marsh. I used to live there as well until I was brought to the castle. The baron has not been back for months and we are starting to wonder what happened to him. Would you know where I could find him, my lord?"

"He left Castle Rye just this day," Roe told her. "I believe he was going back to Lydd. What is it that takes your concern that you would be inquiring about the baron?"

"He left Lydd four months ago, and I need to find him," she said desperately. "You see, I am the baron's wife."

CHAPTER 9

"*Y*ou're his wife?" Sapphire's mouth fell open. "But . . . I'm married to him as well."

The woman looked to the floor but did not react.

"What is your name?" Roe asked the woman.

"I am Alice," she said. "My brothers and I once herded the sheep together on Dungeness." She pointed to the two men with her.

"So, you are not a noble?" asked Sapphire.

"Nay, my lady. Or at least, I wasn't, before I married the baron six months ago and gained the title of baroness. You see, I was once friends with the true Lady of Lydd."

"What happened to her?" asked Sapphire.

"She died in an accident when she fell down the stairs. I was the baron's mistress at the time. He married me, but left the castle shortly afterwards and has not returned since."

"Do you have proof you're married to the man?" asked Roe.

"I have his ring with his crest upon it that he bestowed on me the day we wed." She held up her hand for them to see.

"Were there witnesses to the marriage?" Roe asked.

"Aye. Though he did not wed me in front of the entire castle, my brothers were both present as witnesses. And the priest would vouch for me as well."

"You need to come with us to my castle," said Roe. "Bring your brothers with us, too." He looked at Sapphire. "I think we've just found a way to release you from your marriage to the baron."

* * *

Roe stood in the solar speaking in private to his uncle while waiting for Father Geoffrey to arrive. Sapphire and his mother stood at the opposite side of the room, while the baron's wife and brothers waited for them in the corridor.

"So, you mean to tell me you didn't know the baron was already married when you so generously offered my betrothed to him?" Roe asked his uncle.

"I knew his wife had died, but not that he'd remarried," explained Henry.

"Somehow, I thought you were quite close with the baron. If so, I am sure you would have at least suspected something."

"You sound as if you don't trust me, Roe."

"Nay," he answered, "I don't. I've never trusted you, Uncle, and I am not about to start now."

"Roe," said his mother, coming forward. "Do you think Sapphire will really be able to get her marriage annulled now?"

"I hope so," he answered, feeling happy yet angry at the

same time. "And I hope that bastard gets everything coming to him. He's mistreated not one woman, but two. For all we know, he could have a few more wives out there as well."

A knock came at the door and a guard stuck his head inside the room. "Lords Sexton, the priest has arrived," he announced.

"Send him in," Roe ordered. The door opened wider and the priest walked inside. "Send in the sheepherders and the girl as well," he added.

Alice poked her head into the room, entering slowly, followed by her brothers. Roe wasn't surprised that the baron hadn't even given her a proper gown to wear. She wore a simple plain gown not better than any of his hired help. Her hair was pinned up and she wore a wimple – another mark of the poor. Alice was a baroness, even if in secret, and should have been given proper clothing, a cloak and a headdress at the very least.

"What is this all about?" asked Father Geoffrey, looking around the room and surveying everyone gathered inside.

"Father, I'd like to ask for an annulment for Lady Sapphire," said Roe. "Did you bring the signed marriage parchment from Lady Sapphire and Baron Lydd as I've requested?"

"I have it right here," answered the priest, bringing a rolled-up parchment from under his robe. "But I'm sorry, you cannot request an annulment, Lord Sexton. Only one of the married couple in question can be the one to place the request."

SAPPHIRE HURRIED FORWARD and greeted the priest, then

nodded to the others in the room as well. "I'll make the request then," she told the priest. "I'd like my marriage to the baron annulled since when he married me, this woman was already his wife." She splayed her arm forward, pointing to Alice.

"What are you saying?" asked the priest, confusion furrowing his brow.

"Father Geoffrey, this is Alice, wife of Baron Lydd," said Sapphire. "She's come forward just this day looking for her husband. It seems the baron married her six months ago. That means he was already married when he took his vows with me."

"Is this true?" the priest asked Alice with a frown on his face.

"It is," said the girl shyly. "I have his crest ring he gave me at the wedding to prove it." She held up her hand with the large ring on her thumb.

"Are there witnesses who can vouch for you?" asked the priest.

"My brothers will both confirm it," she replied, nodding at the two men.

"Do you both admit to having witnessed the wedding between Alice and Baron Lydd?" asked the priest.

"We do," they answered in turn.

"This is terrible," said Father Geoffrey. "I never would have performed the wedding had I known. This is why wedding banns are posted three weeks ahead of time. That way, anyone with a reason for the couple not to marry, can come forward. I knew I should have insisted the banns be posted, but the baron seemed to be in a hurry and assured me no one would object."

"So will the marriage be annulled then?" asked Sapphire, holding her breath, waiting for his answer.

"Normally, this is a decision made only by the pope," explained the priest. "However, I don't really want him to know I went against procedure by not insisting on the posting of the banns."

"So you can allow the annulment then?" asked Roe.

"Well, I suppose so. But I'd need to talk to the priest who married them first. I think with that and the witnesses coming forward, it should be sufficient. Was it Father Gerard from Lydd who performed the ceremony?" he asked Alice.

"Aye, it was," answered the woman.

"Then you are in luck," said the priest. "Father Gerard arrived at the castle just this morning from Lydd and awaits me for our monthly meeting and prayer session in the great hall as we speak. Perhaps someone can ask him to join us?"

"Guard," called Roe, and the door to the room opened slightly.

"Aye, my lord?" asked the guard.

"Bring in the priest from Lydd who awaits Father Geoffrey in the great hall."

"At once, my lord," said the man and disappeared.

"Alice," said Sapphire, feeling sad for the girl since she knew how horrible her marriage to the man must have been as well. "Perhaps you can get your marriage annulled, too, while the priests are both here, as well as your brothers."

"Oh, but I don't want to," protested the girl.

"You don't?" asked Sapphire in surprise. "Why not? You can't tell me you love the man after what he did?"

"Nay, I don't," she admitted. "And I think it is no secret he likes to bed many women and beat upon them all."

"I'm so sorry," said Sapphire, laying a hand on the girl's shoulder. "So then, why do you want to stay married to him?"

"Because, my lady, as his wife, I will inherit at least one third of his lands and estate if he should die. I know the baron has many enemies. My hope is to be able to keep the marsh-land for my brothers' sheep to graze if he should somehow die or be killed."

"How are your brothers faring?" asked Sapphire curiously. "Has the wool brought them any money at all lately?"

"Nay, my lady," she admitted. "Smugglers have stolen their last two shipments and my brothers do not even have the tax money due to the baron. I look for him now to plead with him not to punish my brothers or take their flock from them because of their ill luck."

The door opened and a priest walked in.

"Father Gerard," said Father Geoffrey. "Do you remember wedding this young lady to the baron of Lydd six months ago?"

The man looked at the girl and smiled. "How are you Alice?" he asked. "Or should I say Baroness? Yes," he informed him. "I married her to the baron with only these two men as witnesses six months ago. As far as I know, the baron has never even taken the poor lass to the castle to live the life she is entitled as his wife."

"Then that settles it," said Father Geoffrey, dropping the parchment into the burning fire on the hearth. "Sapphire, I have enough proof that the baron has wronged you. I can't say what will happen to him when he shows up, but I can tell you the church will not condone polygamy. As far as God and the church are concerned, you have never been married to the baron at all. As of this day, Lady Sapphire, you are unmarried, and your marriage has been annulled."

Sapphire watched the signed marriage parchment disappear and go up in smoke. With it went the sense of a doomed life. A weight was lifted off her shoulders, freeing her and making her feel so happy she could have shouted out loud. But although the church would now consider her as never having been married, the emotional and mental scars left by this man would never be forgotten.

"Thank you," she said, nodding to the priest. Looking at Roe, she smiled. "Thank you as well, Lord Sexton."

Roe's eyes twinkled and a smile lit up his face. Then he guided the priest to the door and directed the rest of the guests there as well.

"You are all invited to join us in the great hall for a bite to eat. And thank you, Father Geoffrey, as well as you, Baroness." Roe nodded to Alice. "You have made several people very happy today. I assure you, Lady Alice, that you and your brothers have naught to worry about. I plan on capturing the smugglers who stole your wool shipment and I promise I will put them behind bars for a long, long time."

CHAPTER 10

Sapphire walked to the great hall with Roe at her side. He held out his arm and escorted her, with his mother and uncle right behind them.

"I am so happy," she told him as they walked up to the dais. "I feel as if my life is not so dreary after all."

"I noticed you can't stop smiling," he said, nodding to his men and other occupants of the hall. They settled themselves upon the padded chairs made for the lord and lady of the castle. "Father Geoffrey and Father Gerard, please join us at the dais," he instructed.

When they were settled, Father Geoffrey led the prayer for the meal. But when they were about to start eating, Roe stood up and called the hall to attention.

"What are you doing?" asked Sapphire, feeling as if she already knew.

"I want everyone to know you are no longer that bastard's wife," he said in a low voice. Then he looked out at the crowd in the room and spoke. "As of this day, Lady Sapphire is no longer married to Baron Lydd," he announced.

Commotion and talking amongst the people in the room rang out.

"Please," he said, trying to regain their attention. "I don't want to go into details, but their marriage has been annulled by the church. Isn't that right, Father?" he looked over to the priest.

"Aye," said Father Geoffrey. Father Gerard chimed in as well.

"Now I'd like everyone to lift their cups high and drink to Lady Sapphire."

"Lady Sapphire!" someone called out as everyone raised their mugs in the air.

Sapphire felt awkward in this situation, but liked the attention she was getting from Roe.

"And there's more," he said, which for some reason caused Sapphire to feel a slight sense of excitement and anticipation. "As of this day, I'd like to ask Lady Sapphire to marry me and be my wife."

"What?" she gasped, hardly able to believe what she heard.

"That's wonderful," exclaimed Lady Katherine.

"Roe, this is so sudden," complained Lord Henry.

"Sapphire," said Roe, sitting back down and taking her hand in his. His eyes met hers and she felt the connection between them. A warm, happy feeling engulfed her. It was a feeling she'd never had with the baron. "Sapphire, say you'll marry me and be my wife."

"Yes!" she shouted out so everyone could hear her. "I would be proud to be your wife."

"Then it's settled," said Roe, looking over to the priests. "Father Geoffrey, I assure you I will have the wedding banns posted anon for the proper amount of time. I will not go against the procedure of the church."

"Thank you," said the priest. "And I will be happy to marry you when the day arrives."

Sapphire smiled at Roe. "Thank you," she said. "You have made me very happy. I now have hope in my life once again."

"Thank *you*," said Roe. "I am looking forward to being married to you, my little lark. This was the plan between both our fathers from the beginning."

She noticed the playfulness within Roe's eyes and couldn't stop wondering what her life would be like from this day on.

"I want my family to be here for our wedding," she told him.

"I'll send a messenger this day to Blackpool," he answered.

"Please send a missive to my sister, Ruby, and her husband in Sheffield as well. I want her here for my special day, too."

"Of course, my Lady Sexton," he said, leaning over and kissing her on the mouth in front of everyone. Shouts went out and the music started up. Sapphire could feel the excitement spreading throughout the hall.

She noticed Alice smiling as well. Sapphire admired her for her courage and also for her plan to someday make a wrong into a right concerning the baron. The girl had a good chance of getting the marshlands of Dungeness for her brothers after all. With the baron's reputation, it was only a matter of time before his title was stripped from him or perhaps he was killed.

Then Sapphire saw Erin standing in the doorway watching her and had almost forgotten she'd made the girl her handmaid.

"Excuse me," she said, getting up from the table. Roe helped in his chivalrous way by pulling the chair out for her.

"Where are you going?" he wanted to know.

"I need to instruct Erin in her new duties," she answered.

"Can't that wait until the meal is finished?"

"It can," she admitted. "But I don't think she can wait any longer to see Dugald."

"I still don't feel at all certain that we've done the right thing by bringing her here," said Roe. "You do realize her father hates Dugald."

"That'll change in time." She let out a sigh and smoothed down her gown. "Just trust me."

Sapphire made her way down the dais and toward Erin. The girl stood up straight as she approached.

"I am happy for you and Lord Sexton," said Erin, reaching out to take Sapphire's hands in hers.

"Thank you," said Sapphire. "And I am happy you'll be my handmaiden starting today as well."

Erin released Sapphire's hands and dropped her arms to her side. "I've never been a handmaiden before, my lady. I am not sure I'll be to your liking."

"I will teach you all you need to know. But first, I want you to do me a favor."

"Of course, my lady. Anything at all. That's what I am here for."

"Please go to the stables at once and tell Dugald I'll need my horse saddled and ready just after the meal. I plan on riding this afternoon."

The girl's eyes opened wide at the mention of Dugald. "Of course, my lady. I will tell him and return at once."

"Nay. I require you to stay and make certain he prepares my horse as he should."

"But I know naught of preparing a horse, my lady."

"I realize that, Erin. But mayhap Dugald can show you exactly what he does as the lord's stableboy. So please, take your time." Sapphire smiled and winked at the girl.

She understood and shyly looked to the ground. "Thank you, Lady Sapphire. I truly appreciate this opportunity to be at your service."

"Do not thank me," Sapphire told her. "Consider it my gift to you."

"I can never repay you for your kindness."

"Neither do I want you to. Now go. And stop by the kitchen first and take some food out to the stable that you and Dugald can share."

"Aye, my lady." The girl took off at a good pace, and Sapphire felt as if she had done a good deed.

"That was kind of you to do that for Erin," said Roe, walking up behind her.

"Not just Erin, but Dugald as well. I did it because I can tell those two really love each other."

"So you think they've found this true love of which you speak?" asked Roe.

"Perhaps."

"Do you think we will be able to find it as well, Sapphire? After all, you said you no longer have your jeweled dagger. I'd hate to think our marriage would be loveless because of it."

"I do miss my dagger," said Sapphire. "I would feel better to have it at my side. However, I think we can be very happy together even without it."

"Well, I would like to try to bring you that happiness and

love you search for. I see how important it is to you." He reached out and caressed her cheek. "No one deserves the treatment the baron put you through. I will never forgive myself for staying away so long with no word sent home. I feel as if your misfortune is because of my doing. If I had been here, I would have known about the betrothal agreement between your father and mine. I am so sorry."

"It doesn't matter," she told him. "All that matters is that I am free of that awful man and now we can be together. Will you join me in a ride after the meal?" she asked. "I would like to visit that field of flowers you spoke of outside the castle's walls."

"Of course," he said. "It is a very peaceful place and I think you will enjoy it. It is hidden behind the hill and we will have privacy if we should decide we need it."

"Whatever are you saying, my lord? That you would want to deflower me before the actual wedding and amongst the flowers?"

"Sapphire," he said softly, his eyes darting around the room to see if anyone was listening. "We have already lain together and you are far from being chaste."

"I assure you I am only jesting, my husband-to-be. And I look forward to being your wife." She reached up and kissed him ever so gently on the mouth. Though she didn't think anyone was watching, the crowd cheered from behind him.

A wave of happiness flowed through her. She felt as if perhaps her discarded dreams of marrying and finding true love and raising many children could perhaps be found in this lifetime after all.

CHAPTER 11

Sapphire rode her horse over the meadow behind the castle, laughing as she raced with Roe. He led her over a hill and down the other side. As she stopped her horse and took a deep breath, she reveled at the sight before her eyes.

"It's beautiful!" she cried out, seeing the field of purple larkspur and red poppies that cascaded down the hill coloring the land in vibrant hues. "I feel as if this is a secret field where only the fae of the land are allowed to go."

"I told you that you would like it," said Roe, dismounting and holding out his hand for Sapphire to dismount as well. "Now can you see why this is my mother's favorite place?"

"I do," she said, breathing in the fresh, sweet, flowery air all around her. "It seems late in the year for all these flowers to be blooming though."

"Well, for as long as I can remember, this field of flowers has bloomed from late spring well into autumn. I think that perhaps because it is so well protected in this cove is the reason the flowers fare so well."

He put his arm around her as they strolled through the field.

"I feel just like one of these fragile flowers being protected by you – my own personal cove."

"Believe me, darling, I've seen you at your best and you are far from fragile." He reached out and wrapped his arms around her waist and she reached up and put her arms around his shoulders.

"I am very pleased by not only the annulment, but also my betrothal to you," said Sapphire. "I am so happy, that I could just scream."

He reached down and kissed her then, and she felt herself melting in his embrace. Thoughts of their night together at the inn flitted across her mind and her body responded in excitement.

"If you are going to scream, I'd rather give you a better reason for doing it," he said.

"Oh?" she asked playfully. "And what would that be, my lord?"

"Would you like to find out?" He scooped her off her feet and into his arms.

"I would love to find out," she laughed.

He kissed her again and then turned in circles with her in his arms, causing her to become dizzy.

"Stop it," she laughed, kicking her feet playfully, and then laughed uncontrollably as he took his fingers and tickled her under her arm.

"I can't stop," he teased her, acting as if his spirals were out of control.

"I'm getting dizzy," she shouted. He dropped to the ground with her atop him, both of them laughing until they felt drained. The flowers were tall on all sides of them as well as the grass, enclosing them in a private nature chamber of their own. The scent in the field was magical. The blue skies above them were so vibrant with a few puffy white clouds that she felt as if she were truly in the land of the fae.

"No one can see us hidden in the flowers," he said in a sultry voice.

"Are you suggesting we make love right here out in the open?"

"No one will see us, sweetheart, if you are really that modest. And if you haven't noticed, the hall is full of people sleeping together every night and no one thinks twice of stopping an urge even with everyone around. 'Tis a way of life and naught to be ashamed of at all. But I will respect your decision, as I know how modest you pretend to be."

"I don't pretend," she said, laughing and pushing up on to one elbow. "I *am* modest."

He grabbed her arm and pulled her down atop his chest. Once more, the flowers closed in around them, making a private curtain.

Lying on his back, Roe looked up toward the sky. Sapphire was atop him, facing him.

"Kiss me," he said. "I have not been able to stop thinking of that night at the inn ever since it happened. You have no idea how hard it was for me not to touch you lately, ever since I discovered you were married."

"You did touch me," she reminded him. "Or have you forgotten that kiss we shared when you were bathing?"

"I could never forget a kiss from you, my little lark. And that just goes to show that when I'm around you, I am totally out of control of my senses. I am a man with needs. I am here for you and your needs as well."

"I have a need to love and be loved in return," she told him. "I know it is not common to find love in a marriage, but my sister has it, and so did my parents. Did your parents love each other, Roe?"

"I suppose so," he said, pulling her next to him and cradling her head from the ground with his arm. They stared up at the blue sky and white clouds as they talked. "I really don't understand my mother marrying Henry, though. My uncle was the reason I stayed away so long."

"What do you mean?" she asked.

"I never really liked Uncle Henry. Ever since the day I went to his manor house to be trained as a page," he told her.

"Was he mean to you?" she wondered. "Or perhaps did he beat you the way the baron did to me?"

Sapphire felt his grip tighten when she'd mentioned the beatings. The muscles in his arm beneath her head turned rock hard.

"I'll never let him harm you again," he vowed. "And as for my uncle – he didn't beat me but I always felt as if money, or the thought of having money and possessions ruled every choice he made. Sometimes, they weren't always ethical choices either. So when he lost his manor house when the king decided to give it to the baron of the Cinque Ports instead, my father let him come to live at the castle. I always felt he was after everything my father owned. And when my father died, you can see he was right there to sweep in and claim my father's fiefdom as well as my mother."

"But he thought you were dead, Roe. You can't blame him."

"Nay, I only blame myself for that. But I don't really

believe he thought I was dead. While I didn't send a missive home, nor did he try to find out what happened to me either."

"You sound as if you think he married me off to the baron when he knew you'd be returning someday."

"It isn't entirely impossible."

"Why would he do such a thing?"

"I'm not sure. I beg you not to say anything about it, but I don't think Henry is being honest about everything. There is no way he didn't know the baron was already married when he gave you to him. I just don't believe it."

"Your mother seems happy with him."

"Aye, I suppose. But I think he just reminds her of my father, and that's why."

"Do you have any siblings, Roe?"

"I had a brother, but that's all. A younger brother by two years, but he died when the plague swept through the land. My father almost died then, too, but it seems it wasn't the plague that affected him. But ever since then he'd been sickly. I do miss both of them, Sapphire. Immensely."

"I know how you feel," she said, resting her head on his chest. "I really miss my mother as well as the baby brother I never knew. Even though I was only four at the time of their deaths."

"Aye, you mentioned that. It had something to do with those jeweled daggers."

"My father thought they were to blame. Actually, it was my mother's fault she died."

"How can you mean that?" he asked, pulling her closer and kissing her atop the head.

"Well, she told us she'd been greedy and deceitful. After

she bought four daggers, she tried to steal a fifth from the blind old hag."

"Whatever for?"

"She wanted as many children as possible. I guess that's where I get my love for children."

"You want many children?" he asked.

"At least a dozen."

"A dozen?" His head popped up with his eyes wide, making her laugh.

"I'm jesting with you," she said. "I don't need as many children as the queen. I think four or five would be nice though."

"That, I could see," he said. "But a dozen?"

She laughed again. "Anyway, my mother bumped into a beggar boy and she dropped the stolen dagger. The stone cracked. It was a black stone with an orange line running through it. The blind hag realized what was happening and she accused Mother of stealing it. I guess my mother must have pushed the beggar boy away four times because she told us that the blind hag cursed her by saying since she pushed a boy away, all her children would be girls."

"Sapphire, do me the favor of never pushing a beggar boy away because I really want a son someday."

"I promise you, I won't. I want sons as well as daughters."

"Then what happened?" he asked.

"Well, she also told my mother she'd pay for what she'd done. The hag said she'd not only lose a boy child but also her true love. That's exactly what happened when she lost the baby boy she'd birthed and also died that day."

"I'm sorry. I know how hard this must be for you."

"Not only for me, but also my sisters and especially my

father. That's why it's so important to me to have them present at our wedding."

"Sapphire, I promise you that we won't be married until they arrive. But just please don't make me wait to make love with you again until then. Three weeks is a long time for a man to take cold baths and try to ignore his manly needs."

"I agree, and a woman has needs as well as a man. Still, I don't think we should stay in the same bedchamber until after we're wed. It just isn't proper."

"Everyone already knows you're not a virgin, sweetheart. They also realize we are to be married."

"Still, just the same, I think it would look better if we didn't."

"Then we'll have to sneak away to fields of flowers and have trysts to hold us over until the wedding, or I'll go mad from want."

"Don't fool yourself to think you're the only one who'll go mad from want. I think most men don't realize that women have the same needs as men."

"Then let this be our secret spot where we can both find the release from our manly and womanly urges," he told her. He pulled her atop of him and her long hair fell across his face.

"Sapphire?" he said from under her hair. "As much as I love your long locks, I do think when we have our secret trysts it might be advisable to wear it up so I don't suffocate beneath you."

"Your wish will be granted, my lord. But for today, our tryst will have to happen with you holding your breath I guess."

"Do you mean it?"

"That you'll have to hold your breath?" she giggled.

"Nay. About the tryst."

She turned her head and looked around and realized being behind the hill and also down low in the flowers they were pretty much hidden from sight. "I think we'd better hurry before anyone comes looking for us," she suggested.

"Sapphire, you really are not modest, no matter what you say."

He reached up and kissed her, pulling her gown from her shoulders. His hands caressed her breasts while her hands undid his belt and found their way under his tunic.

"Let me help," he said, all but ripping off his hose and braies, not bothering to remove his tunic. Then he pulled her back atop him, lifting her skirts. "What is this?" he asked in surprise when he found she wore no undergarments.

"I have no undergarments thanks to the baron burning them all," she told him.

"Then I'll make certain to have some constructed for you at once. No wife of mine will be walking around half-naked."

"Then enjoy it today, since you'll never see it again," she teased him.

He pulled her legs astride his body and settled her atop him. "You are so beautiful, sweetheart. I look forward to making many babies with you."

She bent down for a kiss and when she did, he slipped his length inside her. A surge of heat rose through her body and she felt the instant stirring of her inner core that she'd felt that night at the inn.

"Roe, I've never done anything so reckless as this," she said in a breathy whisper, rocking her hips atop him.

"Aye, you have," he said, matching her with his thrusts. "I'd say dressing like a tart and making love with a man you'd never met tops this, wouldn't you?"

She felt herself climbing, higher and higher. Throwing back her head in elation, she squealed in delight as she started to reach her peak.

"I like being on top," she told him, riding him as if she were sitting atop a stallion.

"Don't get too used to it," he warned her. "I like being the aggressor. However, today, I give up that right as I would not want you to soil your gown in the dirt."

Their dance of love became faster and faster. A wisp of air flitted across her bare skin from the late summer breeze. Never had she thought she'd be making love in a field of flowers and that it'd be so exciting. She'd found a part of her lately that she didn't know existed. It surprised her, but Sapphire loved the idea of coupling in unconventional places. Her body vibrated, pulling him inside her warmth. Still partially clothed, she felt as free and wild as the flowers that grew without reservation across the ground.

It was as if she were one with nature as the scents from the flowers engulfed her. Through partially closed eyes, she saw the vibrant purple and red of the flowers and the blue of the sky. As she reached the peak of her climax, the colors seemed to intensify.

"Let yourself go," he told her through ragged breathing.

"I feel like I want to shout out," she said excitedly.

"Then do it."

She didn't need him to coax her further as it felt so wonderful that she threw back her head and shouted into the breeze. She'd found her release and he did as well, throwing caution to the wind from beneath her as he cried out his passion, too.

She fell to his side and laid her head upon his chest and, together, they regained their breathing to a steady pace.

"Did we just really do that?" she asked in amazement.

"You are not modest, honey. Now do you believe me?"

They laughed, wrapped in each other's arms. It made Sapphire realize that perhaps she didn't need her jeweled dagger after all because she was sure she'd just found in Roe, her one and only true love.

"WHAT WAS THAT?" asked Baron Lydd, standing in the shadows of a tree and straining his eyes toward the field just beyond the castle. "It sounded like passion, and laughing.

"I didn't hear anything." Lord Henry looked around nervously, not wanting to be discovered by anyone as he met in secret with the baron.

"I see two horses across the field," said the baron. Then he looked closer. "That looks like Roe helping my wife mount the horse. I'll have his head for even touching her like that."

"That's what I wanted to tell you," said Henry. "Now listen closely, since I need to get back before Roe sees me. Your marriage was annulled by the priest today. Roe is now to be Lady Sapphire's husband."

"What?" the baron all but screamed. "How the hell did this happen?"

"You got careless," Henry told him. "And you are a bastard for not telling me you were already married before you convinced me to give you Lady Sapphire's hand in marriage. Your little wife of the sheep showed up looking for you."

"Damn!" he spat. "I knew I shouldn't have married her. I had a weak moment and gave in. But stop complaining," said the baron. "You got half the dowry from Sapphire. If it wasn't for me, you'd have nothing. Besides, you owe me for keeping your secret from years ago about not paying prisage to the king."

"That didn't matter, and you know it."

"Not true. After all, you know as well as I that it is the crown's right to claim one tun of wine from ships transporting ten to twenty tuns. And the king takes two tuns of wine from ships that have twenty or more. You should be happy you weren't operating from a foreign trade ship or you'd have paid coins to the king for every barrel aboard the ship."

"Well, I didn't see that as fair," complained Henry.

"I don't think the king would agree with you. That's why you now pay homage to me for keeping your little secret."

"I wish you had never caught me. If not, I wouldn't be indebted to you today and also at your mercy."

"Well, I could have turned you in and you'd be imprisoned or perhaps missing a hand today for trying to take what by right was the king's. So being at my mercy is the better of the two choices, don't you think?"

"I've paid dearly through the years to silence you," said Henry. "I just want this all to be over. And that's something else I wanted to tell you. Roe is suspicious of us. He knows about the smuggled wool. I don't want to be a part of this anymore. I decided I really love my brother's wife even if I only married her to claim his lands. I didn't think I'd feel this way, but I do."

"We have a shipment right now sitting in the secret tunnels at the Bucket of Blood Tavern. You are not going to back out now. We need to get it on a ship and to France immediately."

"Well, that's not going to happen. Roe has put everyone on alert and is checking every ship that comes in or goes out of port."

"Then bribe the dockmen."

"Not that easy. Roe's put some of his own men to watch the dockmen. There is no way we're going to be able to ship it after all."

"I've already made the deal! I want the money my contacts are willing to pay to get some of this fine English wool. I'll just find somewhere else for the ship to dock when they send it."

"Like where?"

The baron thought for a minute before he answered. Then a smile spread across his face. "Off the marshes of Dungeness. There is a spot where the ship can anchor close to the shore. We'll take the barrels to the ship by rowboat, a few at a time."

"That's preposterous. It'll never work," said Henry.

"We don't have a choice now, do we?" asked the baron. "Now, I'll get the word overseas, and the ship should arrive sometime next week. I'll send you a message to let you know when to meet me at the tavern so we can transfer the shipment. I only hope our coin was enough to keep that damned innkeeper from spilling our secret."

"All right," said Henry. "But after this shipment, I want nothing else to do with you or your damned greed. And when this is over, I never want to see you again."

"Is that so?" he asked. "We'll see about that! In the meantime, if all goes as planned, we can transfer the smuggled goods on Michaelmas Day. Everyone will be celebrating and not paying attention. That day is in a sennight. Hold a huge fair inside your castle walls. When you hear a merchant calling out blackberry pies for sale, you'll know everything is going as planned and that I need you to join us. Understand?"

"Fine. But how are you going to make sure I know it's a message from you and not just another merchant selling pies?"

"No one would ever have blackberries at or after Michaelmas. There is some stupid superstition. But I'll have one of my men pose as a pie vendor and have it on his cart anyway."

"I don't know," said Henry. "It sounds risky. And I don't know about the whole blackberry pie plan as a signal."

"Then I'll make sure you know it's me. Take a bite of the pie and I'll have a message inside directing you to either go to the tavern or to Dungeness, rather than to have someone overhear my man talking with you. I'll make certain the vendor has only one blackberry pie, and sells it just to you. The man who'll be posing as a vendor is Urian. He's always been loyal to me and I'm sure he won't betray us."

"All right," said Henry, once again looking around to make certain no one had spotted him. "Go then, before you're noticed, and I'll await your signal. After that, I wash my hands of all things that have to do with you, Baron. I want none of your deceit within the walls of Castle Rye ever again."

CHAPTER 12

"Ow!" said Sapphire as her new handmaid, Erin, ran a brush through her hair.

"I'm so sorry, Lady Sapphire. I am not skilled at my position of handmaiden. I apologize, and I promise you I will be gentler." Erin was sincere in her apologies and Sapphire couldn't be angry with the girl when she was trying to do her best.

"Nay, you are fine," said Sapphire, taking the brush from her. "Let me show you how it's done. If a lady has long hair such as I do, you need to first brush it from the middle downward and then move upward instead of starting from the scalp. This way it won't become tangled. See?" She gently demonstrated on herself.

"I see now, Lady Sapphire, thank you." Erin reached for the brush and then dropped it, hurrying to bend down and pick it up.

"Erin, you seem to be quite nervous about something," said Sapphire.

"I'm very nervous to be your maidservant, that's all."

"Are you sure there's nothing else that is bothering you?"

"Such as what?" The girl put the brush to Sapphire's hair and, this time, did it perfectly.

"Oh, I don't know. Is everything all right between you and Dugald?"

The girl looked downward suddenly and bit her lip.

"Aye."

"But . . .?"

"'Tis nothing, really," she said, trying to fake a smile but Sapphire could see right through it.

"But what? Tell me."

The girl was silent.

"Erin, I am a woman just like you. We can talk in confidence and I promise I won't tell anyone whatever it is you want to tell me."

"Do you really promise?" she asked with caution in her voice.

"I gave you my word and I will keep it. Now tell me what is bothering you."

"Lady Sapphire, you are so kind. It feels good to have a woman to talk to since I don't have a mother in my life right now."

"Then tell me. Please." She reached out and took Erin's hand in hers, hoping to comfort her and to let the girl know she could trust her.

"'Tis about my father."

"What about your father?" she asked. "Is he ill?"

"Nay," Erin said, shaking her head. "But I think he has perhaps gotten involved with some people of a questionable nature."

"Well, Erin," Sapphire laughed. "He runs a tavern and inn

and has whores working for him with drunkards and gamblers as his patrons. This is expected in his line of work, darling. No one would hold it against him."

"Not just that," she told her. "I heard him talking to someone in the shadows the other night. I didn't mean to pry, honest I didn't. But I couldn't help overhearing what they were saying."

"Really? What did you hear?" asked Sapphire.

"Well, I thought nothing of it at the time, but since your betrothed has been asking questions lately about wool smugglers, I think mayhap there is something to it after all. I believe my father might be in a bit of trouble."

"Erin, are you telling me that you think your father has something to do with the wool that's been stolen? That he has a hand in the smuggling? This is horrible."

"I do. I heard him mention the stolen wool and the Owlers."

"Who are the Owlers?"

"They are the smugglers who use the hoot of an owl to communicate in the darkness of night. I probably wouldn't have thought much of it, hadn't I been grabbed the next morning when I went out back. I was threatened as well."

"What do you mean?"

"My lady, I am so frightened. I never should have said anything to you."

"Come here," said Sapphire, getting up and wrapping her arms around the girl in a motherly hug. "Now, I told you I wouldn't tell anyone your secret so you can confide in me and you don't need to be frightened."

"Someone grabbed me the next morning and pounded

their fist into my face. They told me that if I said anything about what I'd heard they'd kill my father."

"Oh, Erin, that is horrible. Do you have any idea who this person was?"

"It was dark and I didn't see his face, so I'm not sure. But just after that, one of the whores told me she'd seen Baron Lydd outside and wondered why he hadn't requested her services like he normally did when he came to the tavern. She also said she hadn't seen him there the night before and wondered why he was there so early in the morning."

"So Dugald didn't hit you after all, like your father accused him of doing."

"Nay, my lady."

"Did your father know Dugald was innocent?"

"He did. He was trying to protect the baron, I'm sure of it. I didn't want Dugald to get blamed for it, my lady. However, I didn't want my father to look like a liar in front of Lord Sexton either."

"So what do you think the baron was doing there?" she asked. "Are they hiding the shipment somewhere?"

"I don't know, my lady. Now, please don't tell anyone what I said or my father might get hurt or killed. He is the only parent I have, Lady Sapphire, and I don't want to lose him."

"Of course not," she said, running a hand over the girl's back. "I promised you I wouldn't say a word and so I won't. But tell me, Erin, why don't you have a mother?"

"I am ashamed to say my mother was a whore who worked for my father years ago when he first opened the Bucket of Blood. She wanted naught to do with me, and left. It's always been just me and my father all these years."

"I'm sorry," said Sapphire, knowing how hard it must have

been for not only Auley to raise a child by himself, but also for Erin not to have a mother.

Sapphire knew she needed to tell Roe that Auley might be involved in the smuggling, but she couldn't break her word to Erin. The poor girl was so frightened. If what she said was true, her father might get hurt. She couldn't allow that. This girl had only one parent, and Sapphire knew from growing up in the same situation how that felt. She wanted to help this girl and let her know she had someone she could confide in and also trust. She wanted to be the girl's friend.

So she wouldn't tell Roe right now, she decided. But instead, she would try to find a way to investigate this further by herself.

* * *

"YOU SEEM QUIET TONIGHT, SAPPHIRE." Roe strolled through the gardens holding Sapphire's hand. "Is something wrong?"

"Nay, my lord," she answered with a smile. "I guess I am just thinking of our wedding and missing my father and sisters, that's all."

"Well, I sent the messenger today to give the news to both your father and your married sister. I'm sure he will be back soon with a message from them, so just be patient while you wait."

They sat down on the stone bench in the garden and he took Sapphire's hand in his. "Sapphire, sweetheart," he said, "I want to get a ring for you for the wedding."

"That's not necessary," she told him. "Actually, my father sent a sapphire necklace as well as a ring with a sapphire stone in it with me. It used to be my mother's. I haven't been wearing it because I didn't want the baron to steal it, but I think I would like to wear that ring if you don't mind."

"That sounds fine," he told her. "I will still be getting something for you as a betrothal gift. You deserve it, and I want it to be something special."

"That's fine," she said, not even really listening to him. "So, have you heard word of the baron? Has anyone seen him, or has he gone back to Lydd?"

That took him by surprise that she should even be asking about the man she swore she despised. "I don't know," he said. "Why does it matter?"

"Oh, just curious." She flashed a smile. "I thought mayhap he'd show up at the tavern or something, looking for a whore perhaps."

"Did Erin say she saw him at the tavern? I didn't know he went there."

"Nay!" she said almost too quickly. "Erin said naught about the baron. I am the one who wanted to know, that's all."

"Sapphire, you seem jumpy today. Is something troubling you?"

"Of course not." She reached up and kissed him. "What could possibly be troubling me when I am betrothed and about to get married to such a wonderful man?"

He pulled her closer to him and kissed the top of her head. She could say what she wanted, but he had no doubt in his mind there was something she wasn't telling him. Something that he needed to know.

CHAPTER 13

The next day was Sunday, and Sapphire accompanied Roe and the others to mass at St. Mary's church in the village. While she, as well as the rest of the nobles, attended chapel every day, they only went to the church on Sundays and holy days.

When mass was finished, Sapphire walked out the front doors, stopping to admire the piece of parchment hanging there. It was her wedding banns. The banns being posted, made her wedding to Roe seem even more real. Her heart raced, thinking of having children with Roe and someday walking out of mass with her family at her side. This made her happy. She knew Roe would be a wonderful father and she couldn't wait for her own father and sisters to meet him. Her father had chosen a man for her, and she couldn't be happier with his decision.

"Lady Sapphire, what is that?" asked Erin staring at the parchment on the door.

"That is the wedding banns announcing my upcoming marriage to Roe," she explained. Erin did not know how to read or write. It was rare for anyone who wasn't a noble to have this skill, except for the clergy and some of the knights and an occasional merchant. She smiled inwardly thinking how silly it was to post the banns that no one in the village could even read anyway. Mayhap this wasn't such an important custom and procedure after all. Still, she liked it.

"Someday, that'll be you and Dugald," said Sapphire with a smile.

"Oh, I don't know," said the girl. "I don't think my father would ever allow it."

"What won't your father allow?" asked Roe coming to join them.

"It doesn't matter," Erin said quickly.

"Of course it does," said Sapphire. "Erin is concerned that she may never be able to marry Dugald," she relayed the information to Roe.

"Well, well," said Roe crossing his arms and looking at the young girl. "Don't tell me my little Erin has been bitten by the love bug just like my wife?"

"Roe, I am not your wife yet," Sapphire reminded him.

"To me you are. Soon . . . I mean," he added, for Erin's sake so she wouldn't think they'd already been together.

"Your father will never let Dugald marry you if he thinks he's been beating you," said Roe.

"He hasn't," Erin was quick to defend her lover.

"Then who has?" asked Roe curiously.

Erin looked to Sapphire with frightened eyes as if calling out for help, and she knew she had to intervene.

"Erin, can you find Lady Katherine for me and ask her if she'd like to go riding with me later?"

"Of course, my lady," said Erin with a slight curtsy, running off quickly.

"There is something going on here," said Roe suspiciously. "Are you going to tell me what it is or am I going to have to find out for myself?"

"I'm sorry, but there are some things that are just between girls, and I cannot break Erin's trust in me," explained Sapphire.

"Sapphire?" He looked at her and raised a brow. "I am not only Lord of Rye but also your betrothed. And that girl has always been like a little sister to me. If there is something you know, you need to tell me. I will not have either of you keeping secrets."

"'Tis just girl talk," she told him with a peck to his cheek. "I am sure none of it would be of any interest to you. But if I should think something would be to your interest, then I'd be sure to tell you."

She hurried down the stairs and toward her horse feeling terrible for just lying to the man who was soon to become her husband.

* * *

LATER THAT DAY, Sapphire walked into the stable to see Erin kissing Dugald. She stopped suddenly and cleared her throat and the couple quickly darted apart.

"My lady," said Erin, "I am sorry."

"Aye," said Dugald busying himself with brushing the horse. "Your horse is ready, my lady, as well as Lady Katherine's."

"Thank you, Dugald," she said. "I believe Lady Katherine will be here soon."

"I am here now," said the woman entering the stable with her handmaid right behind. "Where would you like to ride today, Sapphire? Perhaps to town or just through the village?"

"I was thinking of riding through the field of poppies," she said. "Roe told me that was always one of your favorite spots to go. 'Tis my favorite now, as well."

They mounted their horses and prepared to leave.

"Shall we come with you my lady?" asked Erin, motioning to the other handmaid.

"I don't think that's necessary," said Sapphire.

"Me neither," agreed Lady Katherine.

"Would you require an escort my ladies?" asked Dugald. "I would be happy to accompany you."

"Nay, not at all. We're not going far," said Sapphire, directing her horse out of the stable.

They rode through the gates and into the field of flowers. Sapphire stopped and dismounted. "I'd like to pick some flowers to bring back to the castle," she said.

"What a wonderful idea," agreed Lady Katherine, dismounting and bending down to help her. "Do you know why I like this field of flowers so much?" she asked.

"Nay," Sapphire answered.

"Because when my husband was alive, this was one of our favorite places to have a secret rendezvous."

"Roe and I rather enjoy it as well," Sapphire answered with a shy smile.

"Don't tell Roe I told you this, but he was conceived in this field on a day just like today."

"Really?" Sapphire wondered if she and Roe would conceive a baby in that field as well.

"I am so happy for you and Roe, Sapphire," said Katherine. "I only wish Roe's father could see what a wonderful union this betrothal has brought about."

"Do you miss him?" asked Sapphire.

"Greatly."

"But you love his brother, Henry, now, don't you?"

"We are fond of each other and I have grown to accept the fact I am his wife, but he will never take the place of my husband, Robert."

Sapphire stood up with her hands full of flowers. She was sniffing them when her eyes fell upon two horses and two men half-hidden in the shadows of the forest, along the edge of the field.

"I wonder who that is," Sapphire said aloud.

"That looks like my husband's horse." Lady Katherine squinted, looking across the field. "But I can't see them clearly enough to know who is with him."

Sapphire knew exactly whom he was meeting in secret. But she didn't have the heart to tell Lady Katherine that her husband was probably part of a deceitful plan that involved the smuggling and also the baron.

CHAPTER 14

*E*veryone was up at sunrise the next morning and gathered in front of the stable, preparing to go on the hunt.

Roe readied his men. He looked forward to hunting in the woods and bringing back the well-needed meat that would line the castle's larder and see them through the winter.

"My lord, how will we be hunting today?" asked the chief huntsman, coming forward to greet Roe.

"Bow and stable, I believe," he told him. "It should be much more productive this time of year."

Bow and stable was a way of hunting where the archers hid amongst the trees remaining stable. Men on horseback with bows and arrows with the hounds leading the hunt would encircle the prey and force it back toward the secluded area where the huntsmen were waiting to make the kill. 'Twas hunting as a team rather than on an individual basis.

"And which hounds would you require, my lord?" asked the kennelgroom, walking up to him with a half-dozen dogs leashed with ropes from their ringed collars up to his arm. "Would you require the mastiffs and alaunts?" he asked.

"Nay. We are not hunting boar or bear this time but rather we will be focusing on the Red Deer. Particularly, the stag. Just bring the running hounds to flush the deer out of the thicket and the greyhounds to take the game down should the huntsmen not make a clean kill."

"My lord, the lymer has found the trail of the deer this morning. It looks to be of a good size." The huntsman displayed deer droppings he'd collected in his hollowed horn for Roe to inspect.

"It looks to be a stag," Roe said as he surveyed by the large droppings. "Hopefully, we'll find more stags than hinds, as that'll be a worthy quarry. Make certain to remind the huntsmen we are targeting the Red Deer. I'll accept the Roebuck as well. However, no hunting of the Roe until after Michaelmas. The same goes for hares, though coneys are fine." Rabbits were fair game any time of year, but there were rules to be followed of hunting certain animals in certain seasons. "And I don't want anyone wasting time with the damned young brockets. We're after the Hart of Ten."

"Aye, we'll look for a Hart of Ten, milord," answered the huntsman.

"Good," he told him. "I want the fifth- or sixth-year size. Let the younger ones grow for next season. So look for their tines to be ten, or near to it, or it won't be worth my time."

The age of the male hart or stag of the Red Deer could be told by the number of tines, or points, on their antlers.

"Aye, milord," the huntsman answered.

"And tell the falconer I'd require half a dozen hawks and falcons as well for the smaller prey."

"Of course, milord." The man bowed and left just as Sapphire walked up with her handmaid, Erin, right behind her.

"So, I hear there is no hunting of Roe today," said Sapphire with a smile. "I certainly am glad because I reserve that pleasure all for myself."

Roe didn't find her reference to his name being a female deer particularly amusing. Still, he had to smile at her jest. He kissed her quickly, and then looked over at Erin.

"Erin, please have Dugald saddle a horse for Lady Sapphire as well as yourself. Also, tell him to pack the net and clubs so I can give my betrothed a fair chance of making a kill."

Often, ladies went along on the hunt. To make the kill easier for them, the deer was usually forced into a net where she would then either shoot it with an arrow or club it to death after the first shot had already been made.

"Oh, no," said Sapphire with a shake of her head. "I don't like killing animals, Roe. I would rather not go on the hunt at all."

"But I'll be gone several days," he told her.

"I understand. I'd like to stay back at the castle, as your mother has suggested we plan the meal for our wedding feast."

"Well, if you're certain," he said, not really wanting to leave her behind. Still, it might be for the best. His hunt would take him to the outskirts of Lydd. Roe planned on stopping there to confront the baron as well as make his way down the marshes of Dungeness to investigate and ask the sheeperders questions about their stolen delivery of wool. So mayhap 'twould be better if she was not along after all.

"Sapphire's not going?" asked Henry, riding up atop his

horse. The man was dressed similar to the hunters in a forest green tunic that fell past his thighs. A hood concealed his head. He wore brown hose. Those were the colors that would blend well into the forest. "Well, I'm not sure I'll be much of a help as I've been feeling ill lately, so mayhap I'll stay behind at the castle as well."

"Uncle, 'tis essential you come along," said Roe. "I was hoping you'd help me question the fishermen and sheep-herders of the Romney marshes about the smuggling that has taken place lately."

"Oh," he said, seeming a bit nervous. "I suppose I'll go then."

"Lord Sexton, the huntsmen and animals are ready to depart," announced his squire, Waylon, coming to join them already atop his horse.

"Fine then." Roe fastened his belt containing his sword and dagger. Extra arrows were mounted on his back. He threw his bow over his shoulder and climbed atop his steed. He then took from his waistband the ivory horn encircled with a gold ring and raised it to his lips, blasting three short notes and held his hand high. "Let the hunt begin!"

Leading the hunting party, Roe made his way over the drawbridge with the entourage right behind him. Lord Henry, and both his uncle's squire as well as Waylon, were at his side. And at the front was a herald holding Roe's banner high. The banner of crimson with a white deer with its hoof atop a bear let others know this was the lord's hunting party and not a band of poachers.

The kennelgrooms held back the dogs while the fewterer ran ahead of them with his hound's nose already to the ground to sniff out the trail of the prey. The falconers followed, as well as the archers on foot. A barrage of servants and pages hurried to keep up from behind them. They carried bags with food and supplies, and led the pack horses that would also be used to carry back the dead prey.

Sapphire watched them leave and then turned toward Erin who was still standing at her side.

"Tell Dugald to saddle horses for us as well as one for himself," she instructed.

"Where are we going?" the girl asked. "I thought you said you were staying here to go over the menu for the wedding with Lady Katherine."

"I will do that, but not until later. I think we need to go pay your father a visit first."

"My father? With Dugald along?" Erin's eyes opened wide. "Oh, nay, my lady, I don't think that would be a good idea. Besides, my father is a late riser. He might not yet be out of bed."

"Then we'll wake him," she said. "I want to arrive when no one is really yet at the tavern. I think if we talk to him together, he might see that Dugald is not a bad person as he assumes after all."

"It won't be safe, my lady. 'Tis close to the docks. We should not be there unescorted."

"You're right," she said. "I'll take one guard to ride along with us, but I'll have to swear him to secrecy. I don't want to anger Roe if he finds out what I've been doing."

Sapphire watched the hunting party disappear down the road. She would miss her betrothed for the next few days. She'd wanted desperately to tell him that Erin's father might

be involved in dealing with the baron regarding the smuggling of the wool, but she'd promised to keep it a secret.
Perhaps she could find out more about this on her own, and if
it was true or not before she would eventually have to break
her promise to Erin after all.

CHAPTER 15

"The hound has caught scent of a deer," said one of Roe's huntsmen, holding back a hound that was sniffing out a trail straight in front of them. "I believe it to be a hart or a stag and it is just ahead."

"Archers, position yourselves at your trees," called out Roe. "Huntsmen, follow along and bring the dogs. But keep them tethered until we spot the prey. Men on horseback, follow me."

Roe led the way on his horse through the woods in the direction the hound had signified. Being on horseback, they had an advantage. The animals they hunted had learned to run from men. However, they did not fear man when he rode atop a horse. He supposed the deer saw no threat in another four-footed animal and therefore trusted them in this position. Roe continued on through the forest with Henry and the others just behind him. Then he stopped upwind of the deer, seeing it through a small clearing munching on leaves. Actually, there was a group of them – one female, several young ones, and one large male.

"Do you see that?" he whispered to Henry.

"Hart of Ten?" his uncle asked.

"I believe it does have ten tines on its antlers," relayed Roe. "This is the prize kill I've been waiting for. The size of it is unbelievable."

Roe waited until the kennelgrooms, huntsmen, and the hounds arrived, then signaled to the men to get their attention.

With his hand in the air, he took another look back at the deer. The female lifted her head, knowing something was amiss. Females had a sense about them and seemed to know things.

"Release the hounds!" he called. His hunters all moved forward in a line, flushing out the deer, moving them back toward the archers hidden in the trees, waiting to make the kill.

Roe loved the chase of the hunt. It made him feel more alive than ever. He charged through the woods with the wind in his hair as he dodged branches expertly as he raced forward, pushing the deer toward its imminent death.

"Remember to leave the hind and the young, he called out. "We want the Hart of Ten only."

The plan worked expertly. They flushed the deer right toward the archers waiting in the trees. Leaves crunched and branches snapped underfoot. White flashes of tails and the back ends of the deer leaping through the foliage could be seen. Then came the rain of arrows, and the thrashing of the stag as an arrow hit its mark, lodging itself into the deer's flank.

Roe stopped his horse and pulled a bow from his back, preparing to make the final shot.

"I've got it," said Henry, pulling his own bow from his back, though he knew it was the lord of the castle's privilege to make the final kill.

"Leave it," Roe instructed, but Henry raised his bow anyway.

Without waiting for him to obey, Roe released an arrow and brought the deer to the ground as the shaft lodged right through its heart.

"I wanted the kill," snarled Henry, spotting the hind and raising his bow to her instead. She had several young ones with her, and Roe worried they would not survive the winter without their mother.

"Lower your bow," he warned him. "She has knobbes with her." Roe could tell the calves were under a year old. If he left the mother alive to care for them through the winter, they would have more meat to hunt in coming years. "Lower your bow I warn you."

"Nay. I'll have a kill on this trip as well." Henry released his arrow and it lodged into the female deer, but his aim was not true and he missed his mark. He hit the back quarters of the hind instead. Frightened and running for her life, the deer took off through the forest.

"Damn you, Uncle!" spat Roe. "I told you to leave it. Now it's injured and we need to follow in order to finish it off before it's found by poachers."

Roe started to follow the deer, but his uncle didn't move. "Henry, I suggest you come with me to hunt down this wounded animal. After all, you are the cause of it. Now, let's go."

"Fine," he spat, showing his reluctance, but following Roe anyway.

Roe couldn't believe his uncle's greediness, nor could he tolerate the way he still thought he was the one to give the orders. He saw something within the man that worried him. He needed to keep a close eye on him as he felt the man could not be trusted.

They traveled far, hunting down the injured deer. It was obviously very frightened and confused as it made its way along the outer perimeter near the coast instead of being swallowed up by the forest. Before he realized it, he found himself on a stretch of land surrounded by the sea on three sides. That is, the pebbled strand of Dungeness just outside of Lydd.

The deer stumbled, and it wouldn't be long before it could go no further. It left a clear trail of blood behind it. Roe decided to put it out of its misery before it suffered any longer. He lifted his bow and shot the arrow that brought the deer to the ground.

"Nay, that was my kill," shouted Henry from beside him, his weapon still raised, but the arrow never having left the bow.

Roe jumped off his horse, noticing the fishermen along the coast and also the sheepherders on the marshes with their flocks. They noticed him as well, and made their way toward him.

Henry saw them, and jumped off the horse. "We need to get the deer out of here quickly and away from these peasants."

Roe pulled his sword from his side and looked at the people coming forward. He recognized Alice's brothers. He also noticed that the herders as well as the fishermen looked gaunt and hungry. He thought how they must be suffering from the loss of their shipment of wool. He still didn't have the answers for them that he'd promised, and had to do something to make it up to them.

"Go to Lydd and see if the baron has returned to his castle," he told Henry. "If so, find out what you can. I highly suspect he is behind the smuggling."

"Nay, I will stay and help you get my kill back to the camp."

Roe shook his head, knowing the man thought he deserved the deer when he didn't.

"You may have wounded the thing, but it is from my forest and I took it down," Roe told him. "As the Lord of Rye, I am making the decision that this deer isn't going anywhere."

"What are you saying, Roe? You aren't really going to leave it for these commoners, are you?"

"They've had a bit of misfortune and lost what would have provided the money to feed them and keep them warm throughout the winter. They are down on their luck, so I will leave it for them in promise that I will find their stolen shipment of wool soon."

"You can't mean that."

"I most certainly do."

"But these people are under the fealty of the baron. He can see to them instead."

"I don't see that happening. Now go to the castle and find out what you can. I am going to offer these poor people this meat. Hopefully, it'll make them trust me enough to tell me anything they might know to give me the answer of not only who stole their goods, but also where the smugglers might be right now."

Henry reluctantly did as ordered, but Roe had a feeling

deep inside that his uncle knew more about the smuggling than he was letting on.

* * *

SAPPHIRE STOPPED her horse behind the Bucket of Blood Tavern, not wanting to be seen entering the front of the establishment – especially this early in the morning. It would not do well for a lady to be talked about going into a place like this. And though she didn't want to bring the guard, she figured she had no choice. She didn't want trouble like the last time she was here.

"Lady Sapphire," said Erin, dismounting. "I really don't think this is a good idea."

"Neither do I," agreed Dugald from atop his horse.

The guard stayed silent, surveying the area. She'd paid him well to not only come to protect them today, but also to keep his mouth shut around Roe. Roe would be furious if he knew she'd come back here, but she had to do this for Erin and Dugald. She knew how much the young couple was in love and she needed Auley O'Conner to know that Dugald was not the woman beater he thought the young man to be.

Sapphire dismounted and Dugald hurriedly followed, taking the reins of all three horses and tying them up to a tree. The guard dismounted and stood a short distance behind them.

They walked into the back door of the tavern that opened into a kitchen. One servant stirred a pot that hung above the fire. She jumped up and curtsied when she saw them.

Sapphire just nodded. "Good morning," she said, finding herself pulling her mantle around her just like she'd done the last time she'd visited this place. "Would you know where we could find Mr. O'Conner?" she asked the woman.

"He is stayin' in the room just at the top of the stairs," said the cook. Sapphire thanked her with a smile and followed Erin through the kitchen with Dugald and the guard right behind. She stopped and turned around.

"You two stay here for now," she instructed. "I'd like to approach the man first with just his daughter."

"That's fine with me," said Dugald, settling himself atop a wooden bench pulled up to a table in the kitchen. The cook rushed over and offered him food.

"I need to stay with you," said the guard. "It is my responsibility to protect you, my lady."

"I'll be fine," she told him. "I don't want Erin's father alarmed by seeing you. Just keep a keen ear and if I am in danger, I will call for you."

"Aye, my lady," he said, and went to stand next to Dugald.

"I'm nervous, Lady Sapphire," said Erin as they walked out to the tavern area and up to the base of the stairs leading to the upper rooms.

"You need to confront your father, Erin. Just tell him how you feel about Dugald and make sure he knows the boy never did anything to hurt you."

"I will, my lady, but please stay with me by my side."

"I am here, Erin," she said with a reassuring smile and a pat to the girl's shoulder.

Sapphire had every intention of climbing the stairs to the room that held Auley O'Conner, but when she looked upward, she froze in her tracks. That was the same room she and Roe had shared after he dragged her up these stairs thinking she was naught more than a whore. It was also the same room where she'd felt for the first time in her entire life completely sated. Her cheeks flushed just remembering it.

"You go," she told Erin. "Bring your father down here and then we can talk. I'll just wait here for you."

"All right," said Erin, looking upward, then climbing the stairs slowly.

Sapphire waited in the tavern area, glad no one was here yet this time of day. She paced the floor and looked around, noticing a dying fire at the far hearth. But at the second hearth, though logs were stacked, 'twas void of fire and looked clean – as if it'd never been used. She heard a creaking sound coming from the hearth and a soft hooting that reminded her of an owl. She was about to investigate when she heard Erin calling her from the top of the stairs.

"He's not here, my lady."

Sapphire lifted her skirts and moved quickly, stopping just at the bottom of the staircase. Looking up into the semi-darkness, she spoke to Erin.

"What do you mean?"

"He's not in the room," said Erin. "He must have already left. I'm not sure where to find my father."

"Erin?"

Sapphire spun around, seeing Auley O'Conner close to the hearth that was void of fire. He was crouching, and stood up and peered through the darkness to see them. It startled Sapphire, since a minute ago no one was in the room, nor did the front door open while she was standing there. 'Twas almost as if the man appeared from thin air. She didn't understand from where he'd come.

"What are ye doing here?" He sounded excited to see her until he laid eyes upon Sapphire. "What's going on?" he asked.

"Why is she here?" His eyes bored into Sapphire, making her feel uncomfortable and unwanted.

"Father, it was Lady Sapphire's idea that we come to speak to you." She descended the stairs and stood next to Sapphire now. She seemed nervous and slightly scared of her own father.

"Well ye need to leave. Both of ye. Now." He oddly looked over his shoulder into the dark room as he said it.

"Mr. O'Conner, I think you need to know that your daughter and Dugald are very fond of each other."

"Don't talk to me about that damned stableboy. I don't want to hear it," growled Auley. "He hurt my daughter and I don't want him near her."

"Nay, I didn't," came Dugald's voice from the door to the kitchen.

"Ye're here, too?" The man didn't look at all pleased.

"Mr. O'Conner, I love Erin," said Dugald. "I promise you, I never hurt her and never will." He walked over and put an arm around the girl.

The innkeeper glanced nervously over his shoulder once again and walked closer, seeming to try to herd them toward the kitchen.

"Fine. I believe ye, now go."

"We want to get married," Dugald added, and Sapphire just held her breath waiting for the innkeeper to explode with anger.

The man looked at them and his eyes narrowed.

"Are ye with child?" he asked his daughter suspiciously. "Because if ye are, Erin, I'll kill the damned boy with my own hands."

"Father! Don't say that," exclaimed Erin. "And nay, I am not with child but we would like to have children someday."

"That's right, Mr. O'Conner," said Dugald. "We would like your permission to get married."

"What!" His eyes opened wide and his face reddened. He obviously was not fond of the idea.

"Erin, ever since yer mother left us, I have raised ye by myself. We have always been together, just the two of us."

"I know," she said, running to him and throwing herself into his arms. She buried her head against the man's chest. "I love you, Father, but you need to let me go. I am a woman now and want to someday have a family of my own."

He was choked up and his eyes looked glassier than before. Slowly putting his arms around her, he shook his head in defeat and looked over at Sapphire.

"This is all yer doing, isn't it? First ye take her away from me to work at the castle and now ye are going to take her away from me forever."

"That's not true, Father," Erin broke in. "Lady Sapphire has been nothing but kind to me. Being by her side, I have felt for the first time that special bonding of two females that I had never known with Mother. She brought me here today because she knows how important it is to all of us that you accept us and our idea of getting married."

"That's right," agreed Dugald.

"Lady Sapphire is the only person I've ever met who believes a marriage should be based on love," added Erin.

"All right then," he finally said. "Ye can be betrothed for now, but I want ye to wait for a while yet before ye get married."

"Oh, thank you, Father." Erin hugged her father and Dugald came over to thank him as well.

Sapphire heard that noise again coming from behind the innkeeper. It sounded like wood and stone sliding or scraping.

"And once again," said Dugald. "I never hit your daughter."

"I believe ye," Auley finally said with a nod, accepting the boy.

"Well, well, well, what do we have here?" Sapphire looked up to see the baron emerging from the shadows behind the innkeeper. Her body stiffened and her heart beat quickly. This was the last person she'd hoped to see. "My little wife has returned to my side after all."

He walked forward and reached out, gripping Sapphire by the chin. She pushed his hand away and took a step backward.

"I am no longer your wife," she told him. "The marriage has been annulled and I am betrothed to Roe now."

"Aye. So I've heard, though I can't say I like it. What are you doing here?" he asked her. "And so early in the morning?"

"I could ask you the same question," she answered boldly.

"Father, why *is* the baron here?" asked Erin.

The man got a harsh warning stare from the baron, and he seemed to be taking his time to answer.

"He just wanted a girl for the night," Auley said. "That's all."

"You seem to have had all the girls you can get," retorted Sapphire. "I find it odd you are Baron of Lydd but you spend so much time in Rye. Why don't you go back to your wife, Alice? She was in here looking for you, you know. And I see you gave her a ring – something you never gave me. Perhaps there is love for a woman in your heart after all? Or mayhap you are just using her like you used me, treating us no different than whores."

That angered him and he stepped forward and gripped her

147

by the arm. His face came closer to hers and he growled out his reply in a low voice.

"You bitch! Well, I suppose you'd know about being a whore since you coupled with Roe right in this very place while you were married to me. Don't think everyone here didn't know it was you hidden beneath the cloak."

"Leave me alone," she cried, trying frantically to pull out of his grip.

"Walter, let the girl be," said Auley.

Sapphire saw Dugald stepping forward to protect her, and she raised her hand in warning to stop him. "Nay, Dugald, don't get involved." Then when the baron's other fist started to raise and she was sure he was going to hit her, she shouted out, "Guard, come quickly."

The guard was there instantly, the sound of his sword being pulled from the scabbard echoing through the room. The baron released her arm and stepped back with his hands raised slightly.

"Is there a problem, my lady?" the guard asked, and she thanked the stars now that she had brought the man along for protection.

"There's no problem," said the baron with a sickening smile on his face.

"Let's go," Sapphire told Dugald and Erin. And in a walk that she wanted to turn into a run, she made her way out of the building through the kitchen with her entourage right behind her.

Sapphire pulled herself up into her saddle quickly, her body shaking inside just from being near the baron. What was he doing here? And what was that noise she had heard by the hearth? How did the baron and the innkeeper seem to have just appeared from nowhere? She didn't know at the moment and was too upset to even think. What made her even more nervous was the fact that she knew now that she needed to tell Roe about this, and she was going to have to break a promise to a young girl who meant the world to her.

CHAPTER 16

*N*early three days later, Roe returned from the hunting trip, hot and tired. He'd swum in the lake this morning, which cooled his body but not his anger toward his uncle and the way he'd acted. Henry had told him the baron wasn't at Lydd. If Roe had trusted his uncle, he wouldn't have had to waste the time in going to see for himself. But sure enough, the baron was nowhere to be found. He wondered where the bastard was hiding.

The hunt had been very successful. They'd fell several Harts of Ten, as well as small game like rabbit, squirrel, and pheasant. The falconers had done their part as well, as the hawks had brought in extra food in the forms of ducks, geese, crows, and a few pigeons.

Even the hounds were helpful and very happy with all the entrails and scraps from the kills with which they'd been rewarded for doing their part in the hunt.

"Did you find out any information about the smugglers while you were in Dungeness?" asked his squire, Waylon, from his side.

"Aye, do tell." Henry interrupted, riding his horse up next to him to join in the conversation. "You never did reveal to me what the fishermen and sheepherders told you, Nephew."

Since Roe didn't trust his uncle, he'd been quiet about his findings. While the sheepherders hadn't told him much, he still had his suspicions. More than one of them had said they'd seen Henry on the marshlands lately, and that didn't sit well with Roe at all. He decided not to mention it. Instead, he fed his uncle some other information to see how the man reacted.

"Well, I did find out that someone with money paid the sheep shearers dearly to pack up the wool in barrels and load it aboard a cart a day ahead of schedule. They came forward and admitted to it, but they thought it had been orders from the baron. Of course, they said the baron had said later that the order wasn't given by him."

"That's odd," said Henry.

"Aye," said Roe. "They also said the baron hasn't been seen much at all in the last four months. We both know that's because he'd been living in Rye with you."

"Just visiting," Henry corrected him. "Just visiting, that's all."

"It seems odd he'd find more to do in Rye than he would in running his own castle. Something must have been of major importance to keep him here – near the docks," he added as an afterthought.

"Well, he was married to Sapphire, so that's why he was at Rye."

"Aye, and I still don't know why you let him marry her in the first place."

"I told you, Roe. We thought you were dead."

"Well, we all know now why he didn't take his new wife

back to Lydd," Waylon added. "That is, because he already had a wife waiting for him there."

"Uncle, you do realize now that I am betrothed to Sapphire, you are going to have to give up her dowry."

"I only have half the dowry," Henry reminded him. "Much of it has already been used or spent. The baron actually has most of it, Roe."

"Then I trust that you'll contact him for me someday and get that returned to me as well."

"Of course," he said, unconvincingly. "If we ever find him."

"Oh, I have a feeling he'll show up sooner or later," said Roe. "After all, greedy men like him are not able to stay hidden and quiet for long."

"So, do you think he's been smuggling the wool?" asked Waylon.

"I do," Roe admitted, "among other things. And I am willing to bet he has several accomplices helping him." He looked at Henry. "People that we might even know or that reside within my castle walls."

"Do you really think so?" asked Henry. "Nay, I don't think anyone at Castle Rye is involved."

They approached the castle and before they even got over the drawbridge, a guard from the gatehouse hurried up to Roe's side.

"My lord, I need to talk to you anon."

"Speak," said Roe, continuing to ride as the man ran along-side him.

"I don't want to betray your betrothed, Lord Sexton, but I need to let you know that while you were away, I accompanied her to the Bucket of Blood Tavern."

"What?" He pulled on the reins and stopped his horse.

Waving his hand, he signaled for the rest of the hunting party to continue on into the castle. Henry, of course, didn't leave his side.

"She took that stableboy and her handmaid with her to talk to the innkeeper," continued the guard.

"What the hell is going on?" he spat.

"She convinced the innkeeper to agree to let the young couple be betrothed."

"Really?" asked Roe. A sense of admiration filled him that Sapphire was such a good matchmaker and also a mediator. She held care and concern within her heart and would someday make a wonderful mother as well. Still, she shouldn't have deceived him. And the last place he wanted to find out she'd been, was at the Bucket of Blood Tavern. "It's dangerous for her to be near the docks. Why the hell did you even let her go?"

"Here, my lord." The guard handed him a small pouch. "She paid me to keep quiet, but I had to tell you."

"Thank you," said Roe, fingering the pouch of coins. "You did the right thing." He took the pouch and tied it at his side.

"One last thing, my lord. I had to protect her when the baron grabbed her and was about to hit her."

"The baron?" Roe's eyes shot over to his uncle. "So that's where the hell he was."

"The baron at the Bucket of Blood?" asked Henry. "That is odd, indeed."

"What do you think he was doing there?" Roe asked his uncle.

"Surely, I have no idea."

"Well, I have an idea, and I am willing to bet it has something to do with the smuggling."

"Ah, that explains it," said Henry with a nod of his head.

"It explains that what I said about him having an accomplice is true." He stared directly at Henry. The man's face froze and he looked to be biting the inside of his cheek.

"How so?" he asked.

"The innkeeper," said Roe, and watched as the man's face relaxed and his shoulders dropped, too.

"Aye, that sounds feasible. They must be in this smuggling ring together."

"Did Lady Sapphire get hurt?" Roe asked the guard.

"Nay, my lord. I brought her back to the castle immediately."

"Thank you for watching over her while I was away," Roe said, pulling a coin from the pouch the man had just given him. He handed it to the guard for his loyalty. He then directed his horse, once more, over the drawbridge. He knew now why Sapphire had not wanted to go along on the hunt. And she was going to have hell to pay as soon as he saw her.

* * *

SAPPHIRE RAN across the courtyard quickly to meet the hunting party returning through the castle gates. Everyone was excited and rushed over to meet them. It had been nearly three days since she'd last seen Roe and she missed him immensely.

"My lord," she said, walking alongside his horse until he stopped. "How was the hunt?"

He dismounted and gave the reins of the horse to Dugald who rushed out to join them.

154

"The hunt went well, but not as productive as your own I'll wager."

"Roe?" she asked with a slight giggle, reaching up and kissing him. She had hoped he'd take her in his arms, but he was acting cold toward her. "What do you mean?"

"Did anything happen while I was gone?" he asked.

Her eyes flitted over to Dugald who had started to say something. She cleared her throat in order to warn him to keep quiet. Then she returned her attention to Roe. "Nay, not really. Nothing out of the ordinary."

"What did you do while I was away?" he asked.

"Oh, not much," she said with a shrug, wondering why he was acting so oddly. "I planned the wedding meal with your mother. And now that you have all this glorious food from the hunt, I see we will have to change it."

"Is there anything else you want to tell me, Sapphire?"

She tired of his game and would not play it any longer.

"Why don't you just come out and tell me what is bothering you, my lord?"

"Well, let's just say congratulations are in order to you, Dugald." He looked toward the boy. "I hear you are betrothed to Erin."

"Thank you, Lord Sexton," the boy said with a large smile.

"I wonder if the baron was happy about it as well as Erin's father?" Roe made it a point to say this, and it almost sounded as if he knew her secret.

Dugald looked over to her with wide eyes, and she dismissed him, knowing how uncomfortable this was for him.

"Dugald, take the horse to the stable to rub it down, please," she said.

"Aye, my lady." He hurried away from there and she couldn't blame him.

"Why are you keeping from me the fact you went back to the Bucket of Blood while I was gone?" Roe pulled a pouch of coins from his belt and shoved it into her hand.

She stared at the bag, realizing 'twas the same one she'd given the guard in order to keep him quiet of her whereabouts. This was how Roe knew, and there was no sense in denying it now.

"I only wanted to help make amends between Dugald and Erin's father," she explained, hoping to make things better. "I knew how much in love Dugald and Erin were and that they'd never be married if someone didn't step forward to help them."

"You had no right to do that, Sapphire. Just mind your own business from now on."

"As lady of the castle, it is my business," she told him.

"And as you reminded me not long ago, we are not married yet, darling. So you are not lady of the castle yet. When were you going to tell me you saw the baron at the tavern and that he'd almost accosted you?"

"You haven't given me the chance," she retorted, not liking the way the conversation was going between them.

"That was a stupid move, Sapphire. You could have been hurt or even killed. I don't want you leaving these castle walls again without me. Do you understand?"

"So now I'm to be a prisoner here? This is starting to sound no different than when I was married to the baron."

"Don't even compare me to that bastard. And I don't like the fact that my wife is proving to be nothing but a liar."

"A liar?" That cut Sapphire to the bone. She was so upset

by it that she turned and ran across the courtyard, holding back her tears.

"Sapphire, come back here," she heard Roe call from behind her, but she didn't stop. She needed to get away from him and think things over. She had thought things were wonderful between her and Roe but now she wasn't so sure. Her mother had told Sapphire and her sisters that they'd one day find true love and she thought she had found it even though she'd lost the jeweled dagger years ago. But now she was starting to wonder if she was somehow cursed just like her mother.

She ran to the solar that she alone occupied and flung herself onto the bed. Burying her face in her arms, all she could think of was home. Sapphire missed her father and her sisters. Gone were the comfort and the laughter. She was far from her family and felt so sad and all alone. She needed someone to talk to and only wished her mother was still alive.

A knock came at the door and then the sweet voice of Lady Katherine calling out, "Sapphire? Are you in there?"

"Come in," she called out and sat up on the bed drying her eyes with the long tippet of her sleeve.

Lady Katherine came into the room and closed the door quickly. However, Sapphire could see that Roe had been standing right behind her.

The door opened and in he marched. Sapphire once again hid her head in the pillow. "I don't want to talk to him," she said.

"Sapphire, we need to talk," came Roe's low voice from behind her.

"Nay!" she shouted, still keeping her head hidden.

"Roe, I think it's best if you leave us for now," instructed his mother.

"Mother, she is my betrothed and I will not leave."

"As your mother, I am telling you to leave anon, Son. This is going to be a private conversation between two women, so remove yourself from the chamber at once, I beg you."

She heard him sigh deeply and slowly leave and close the door. At the sound of the click, Sapphire sat up and turned around to face Lady Katherine.

"Come here, darling," said the woman, reaching out for her. Sapphire could hold back no longer and burst out into tears.

Neither of them spoke for a few minutes. Lady Katherine continued to rock Sapphire in her arms, while smoothing a hand over her back. It felt so good and comforting. Sapphire could vaguely remember her mother doing this to her many years ago when she was just a child.

"I miss my mother," she said in a soft voice, her head pushed sideways against Lady Katherine's shoulder.

"You have had a hard time ever since you came from Blackpool," the woman said in a calming voice. "But I am here for you, darling, so don't you ever forget it."

"Thank you," she said, pulling back and drying her eyes with the back of her hand. "I feel so silly for crying, but I have always been emotional. You have no idea how much this means to me, Lady Katherine. I have felt so lonely ever since I left my father and my sisters."

"Roe is a good man," she told her. "He loves you. I can tell. He will take good care of you, Sapphire. You don't need to worry."

"I know you are right."

"Then why is it you are crying when you should be smiling? After all, you are getting married in a few short weeks." She reached out and ran a hand over Sapphire's hair in a doting manner. It was naught but a small, comforting gesture, but Sapphire liked it.

"Oh, Lady Katherine, Roe thinks I am naught more than a whore and a liar."

"Nay, don't say that."

"'Tis true. When I was married to the baron, I was so unhappy that I often sneaked out to the Bucket of Blood."

"I know. I told you that I saw you going."

"Well, what you don't know is that on the night Roe returned from overseas, he thought I was naught more than a whore with the disguise I wore."

"Oh, I'm sure that's not true."

"He took me upstairs to a room and made love to me and tried to pay me," she explained.

"Oh, my!" Her eyes opened wide. "I see what you mean."

"I know I should have stopped him from laying with me, but I felt like I would never know elation from coupling nor would I ever know love being married to the baron. This was the only chance I'd ever have. Besides, we all know Baron Lydd is barren, so I would never have the children I wanted either."

"So you coupled with Roe in order to have a child?" she asked in astonishment.

"Nay. I did it because it felt so wonderful that I could not bring myself to stop."

"That doesn't make you a whore, Sapphire. Do not blame yourself for wanting to feel alive. You are lucky, as many women never find that feeling in an entire lifetime."

"I know you're right," she said. "And I'm thrilled to be getting married to Roe. However, I did sneak behind his back to the tavern while he was gone, but only to enable Dugald and Erin to be married."

"Well, then there's nothing wrong with it, even if he thinks there is."

"The baron was there," she told her. "He would have beaten me if I hadn't paid a guard to come along to protect me and keep my secret. Even though he didn't."

"You need to be careful, Sapphire. You could have been killed."

"The only reason why I didn't tell this to Roe was because of a promise I made to Erin."

"What was that promise?" asked Katherine.

"I told Erin I wouldn't say anything, but I just have to tell someone. She thinks her father has something to do with the smuggling and that the baron is involved."

"Oh, Sapphire, you have to tell Roe."

"I can't. I promised Erin that I wouldn't expose her father. She has only one parent and I know how hard it is. She loves him, as he is the only family she has."

"I understand, but if he did something wrong, he needs to be punished," said Katherine.

"We don't know for sure that he's involved," Sapphire told her. "But I have a suspicion, because when I was there, I heard a noise. I think it was the opening of a secret passageway under the tavern, and also what sounded like the owl call used by the smugglers."

"You really need to tell this to Roe."

"I don't know what to do," she said.

"Do what is right. Turn the man in."

"Even if it is going to hurt and take away from someone the person they love?"

"I believe so."

"Well, you might want to reconsider, Lady Katherine, because I have something else to say that could just change your mind."

"Nothing could change my mind, no matter what you say." The woman shook her head stubbornly.

"Are you sure?" she asked. "Because I believe they have another accomplice as well. And I do believe that man is none other than your own husband."

Lady Katherine's face clouded over as she shook her head in denial. "Mayhap we need to find out more information before we mention this to my son after all."

"I agree," said Sapphire with a smile. "Perhaps you can help me."

CHAPTER 17

Several days passed and although Roe had tried to make amends with Sapphire many times, she was avoiding him. She didn't want to be called a liar when he started asking questions that she didn't want to answer.

Since she had her own solar by her request at the betrothal, it was a little easier to not get into a situation where they were bound to end up making love. While she missed coupling with him immensely, she felt as though she needed to find out more information about the smuggling possibly happening at the tavern first. She didn't want to accuse Erin's father, nor Lord Henry, until she knew for certain that they were involved. And until she was sure, she didn't want to be in intimate situations with Roe where he might confront her regarding this issue.

Lady Katherine had kept quiet as well, and they were trying to figure this out together. However, nothing had happened lately that seemed suspicious. She knew she needed to get back to the tavern to see if there were any secret passageways. However, Roe had kept such a close eye on her that she couldn't have sneaked out even if she wanted to.

Roe and Sapphire walked to the courtyard arm in arm. They'd attended mass this morning, and just finished the Michaelmas feast of roasted goose. 'Twas always a tradition to have goose on the feast day of the archangel, Michael. 'Twas a celebration of the protective warrior angel as well as of the first days of autumn. The reaping of the crops to be used for the rest of the year from the fields also happened upon this day.

"Sapphire, you seem as if you're trying to avoid me lately." She could hear the tension in Roe's voice.

"Really?" She faked a smile. "Why would you say that?"

He took her in his arms and kissed her. She found it hard to deny her body's reactions and wanted more than anything to make love with him again. Patience, she told herself. She would hopefully find all the answers she needed soon and once more be in his bed and then be able to answer any questions he might ask.

"Because we've not made love since I've returned from the hunting trip, and I don't need to tell you how much I've missed you."

He pressed up against her, enabling her to feel the bulge beneath his tunic. A wave of heat coursed through her and she realized that she could ignore him no longer. He was soon to be her husband and she didn't want to frustrate him. She felt that same frustration and realized things needed to change between them. She admitted to herself that she had been wrong and childish in staying angry with him. Perhaps she just needed to let things happen, and deal with the circumstances as they arose.

"I've missed you, too, Roe, and I am sorry that we quarreled."

"I'd be willing to make amends with you right now, my little lark. How about we make a quick visit to the solar?"

Sapphire looked around at the hustle and bustle of the courtyard. Today was a huge festival day and people from afar came to a fair that Roe had set up right there in the castle courtyard. A high pole with a large glove staked atop it was displayed just outside the castle gate, denoting to everyone from towns around that this was the meeting place for all to come to sell their wares and celebrate Michaelmas.

Merchants' carts lined the courtyard as they called out their wares to passersby.

"Fish for a penny," called out a fishmonger.

"Candles of beeswax and also tallow," called out the chandler, as they tried to outshout each other.

Jugglers wandered through the courtyard and alewives snaked through the crowd with large trays full of tankards filled to the brims held high upon their shoulders. The ale sloshed over the sides of the mugs and down to the tray as they walked.

"Taste my sweet pies," called out another.

"Come to the mews to see my performers reenact the lord's hunt," called out a man in a costume with fake deer antlers atop his head. Two more performers, one dressed like a huntsman and the other like a hound, were acting out a scene from the hunt in pantomime.

"Flower for your lady?" A woman with a basket of flowers walked up to them. Roe picked out a daisy and handed the woman a coin. He broke off the stem of the daisy and tucked the flower behind Sapphire's ear.

"What do you think, sweetheart?"

"Thank you for the flower, Roe, but we can't leave right now. The courtyard is so crowded with merchants and knights and serfs that we need to be here. This is an important festival day and we represent nobility and order. You are Lord Rye and I am soon to be Lady Rye. It could be quite embarrassing if someone were to see us slip away for a tryst at a time like this."

"I suppose you're right," he agreed. "And I see the reeve signaling to me from across the courtyard. Today is the day I need to collect rents and unpaid debts from the villagers. I also need to see that the fields have been harvested properly and fully and that the castle's share of food for winter is stored away."

"Mayhap tonight when the festivities end, we could make our amends then," she told him.

"I can barely wait." He ran his hands close to the sides of her breasts as he pulled them away.

"You are going to make me into a wanton woman if you don't stop your teasing."

"I am already a wanton man so you'll be in good company. Sapphire, I see my mother across the courtyard. Today is the day we hire new servants. I want you to assist her so you can see how it's done."

"Of course," she said. "I will see you later." She reached up and kissed him again, only to be interrupted by the voice of an old woman sitting on the back of a merchant's cart. She was surrounded by pies of many shapes and sizes.

"Blackberry pie, my lord and lady?"

Sapphire's head snapped up as she surveyed the old, wrinkled woman with her hand outstretched, a small palm-sized pie within it.

"No charge for a lord," she said.

"Oh, thank you." Roe reached out to take it, but Sapphire grabbed his hand and stopped him.

"Nay," she told him. "Blackberries are cursed and not to be eaten from Michaelmas until the spring."

"That's nonsense," stated Roe.

"Nobody will take your pie, old woman," Sapphire told her. "Don't you know that this is the day when Lucifer fell from heaven and landed on a briar patch of blackberries? He spit on them and they are cursed. Only bad luck will come to those who eat of them from this day until they grow again next year."

"That is ridiculous," Roe told her. "'Tis not real, but only a superstition." He reached again for the pie, and Sapphire stopped him once more.

"Please, Roe, don't eat it. I do not want anything to curse our upcoming marriage."

"Alright, sweetheart. For you, I will give up my favorite pie in all the world. Because, I love you and want our marriage to be happy and prosperous, not cursed."

"I love you, too," she said, her heart having wings to hear Roe actually say he loved her out loud. And even in front of a stranger.

"You two are to be married?" asked the old woman, putting the pie down at her side. She raised her face to them. In the sun, Sapphire could see the cloudiness of her blind eyes.

"We are," said Sapphire. "The banns have already been posted. I am to marry Lord Sexton soon."

"You sound as if you two have found true love," the woman surmised.

"I don't know much about love," Roe admitted, "but I would say that yes, I have found true love with my betrothed, Lady Sapphire."

"Sapphire?" the old woman asked. "That is an odd name is it not?"

"I was named after the sapphire stone in a dagger," Sapphire told her.

"You were?" the hag asked curiously, fingering a pouch at her side. "And why was that?"

"Oh, it's a long story," Sapphire said casually.

"Another of her crazy superstitions," added Roe.

"You don't believe in superstitions?" the woman asked him in a crackly old voice.

"Nay. Not really," he admitted.

"Lady Sapphire," said Erin, coming to join them. "Lady Katherine requests your presence as she has a line of people waiting for an audience with her, wanting to be hired to work at Castle Rye."

"Go on," Roe told her. "I need to leave for the village anyway, and I am already behind schedule. I will see you later, my love."

ROE WATCHED Sapphire hurrying through the crowd with Erin right behind her. His mother sat high upon a wooden dais, looking out over the crowd of villagers from many towns vying for the few servants' positions that were available. Henry stood there as well.

"Lord Sexton," said Waylon, making his way through the

crowd and stopping at Roe's side. "The reeve says he awaits you and the day is getting late."

"I am going right now," said Roe, turning to leave, only to be stopped by the voice of the old woman.

"You love Sapphire, don't you?" she asked.

"Aye," he answered, "I do."

"I can see that," she said.

"Old woman, you are blind. I doubt you really meant that."

"Even the blind can see, but in different ways," she told him. "I look into the souls of people, as eyes are not needed for that."

"Lord Sexton, the reeve is heading toward the gate already. Shall I tell him you will be delayed?" asked Waylon.

"Nay," he said. "Tell him I will be right with him."

His squire left and Roe looked back to the old woman. "Do you really believe that blackberry pie is cursed? Is that something you can see with your blind eyes as well?"

"I believe it is, my lord. The one who eats it will no doubt have the devil after him. And I believe in superstitions, too. Did you know you should give your beloved a betrothal gift? It is proper if you really love her as you say you do."

"How did you know I didn't get her anything yet?"

"As I told you, I can see into a person's soul. I also have a gift you can give her that I think she will like."

"What might that be?"

She reached into her pouch and held out an ornate, two-toned, etched dagger with a blue sapphire stone in the hilt.

"That is beautiful," he said, taking it into his hands to inspect it. "I do believe you are right. She spoke of a dagger similar to this that she had as a child."

"Part of that superstition of which she spoke?" asked the woman.

"Aye, it was. I would love to give this to her as I think it would make her very happy. How much do you want for it?" He reached to his pouch of coins to pay her.

"Nothing," she said.

"Really, I can't take such an expensive item for free. Now how much, old woman?"

"The merchants on the feast day of Michaelmas are supposed to give a portion of their earnings to charity in exchange for a space in your courtyard, are they not?"

"They are," he said. "But just a portion."

"Well, consider this my portion to charity and give it to your wife."

"You could make more from selling this dagger than you ever could selling those pies."

"True," she said. "But the pies aren't mine. And the price someone will be willing to pay for this blackberry pie alone will be more than even the value of that dagger."

"Lord Sexton," said Waylon, now with the reeve at his side. "We are ready to accompany you to the village, my lord, as there is much to be done today. We also look forward to making merry at the celebration afterwards."

"Of course," he said. "Just let me pay this old hag for the dagger, first." He turned to try to pay her, but the back of the cart where she'd been sitting was now empty, with only the lone blackberry pie in its place.

"Did you see where she went?" asked Roe, searching the area around the cart with a glance.

"Nay," said Waylon, and the reeve just shrugged. "Oh,

blackberry pie, my favorite," said the squire reaching out for it.

"Nay!" Roe grabbed the boy's wrist and stopped him from taking it. He looked around the courtyard and had an eerie feeling in the pit of his stomach. "Leave the pie," he said, turning and directing his squire toward the gate. "We have duties to attend to and no time for that. Besides . . . don't you know that if you eat blackberries on Michaelmas that you will be cursed by the devil?"

The boy just looked at him oddly and Roe felt like a fool for actually saying that aloud. But for some reason, he actually believed the damned superstition now. And he didn't need anything cursing his wedding to Sapphire. He took the jeweled dagger and secured it into his weapon belt, anxious to give it to Sapphire. He would do it tonight, just as soon as they were alone.

CHAPTER 18

"Sapphire, hurry," said Lady Katherine as Sapphire climbed atop the raised wooden platform and stood next to her as well as the steward. "We have a long line of villagers and serfs to talk to in order to decide which ones will serve us the best."

"Aye," said Henry, from the foot of the platform. "Where have you been?"

"I am sorry," she said. "I was distracted by a blind old hag selling blackberry pies." Sapphire took the flower from her hair and sniffed it, thinking of the wonderful time she'd soon be spending with Roe.

"Blackberry pies?" asked Henry, suddenly curious. "Where was this? I need to find this person immediately."

"Why, right over there," said Sapphire, pointing to the cart. She noticed that the old woman was gone but a man who looked more like a dock rat than a merchant stood at the back of the cart instead. He was dressed in ragged clothing and had a woolen cap with a turned-up brim covering his head. "I see that cursed blackberry pie from here. Whatever you do, don't eat it. I can't believe someone would even bring it to Michaelmas. The nerve of them as they know as well as everyone that blackberries this time of year are naught but the work of the devil."

"I need to leave now," said Henry, which got a negative reaction from his wife.

"Henry, you promised to stay and help oversee the hiring of the new servants. And we were going to stroll through the gardens together right afterwards."

"Nay, I can't. I'll be gone the rest of the day so don't wait for me."

"Where are you going, Husband?" she asked as the man hurried toward the cart.

"Don't worry about it, dear. I have something I need to tend to."

Sapphire watched as Lord Henry hurried over to the cart and conversed quickly with the man. He paid him a coin and picked up the pie and took a bite. Then he pulled something out from inside the pastry that looked like a small piece of parchment. He wiped it off and read something on it, then shoved it into his pouch, and headed away. Sapphire noticed the parchment fall out of his pouch as he headed for the stable.

She put her flower down on the chair, all the while keeping her eyes on the piece of dropped parchment. "I'll be right back," she told Lady Katherine and rushed through the crowd, dodging people until she got to the cart. She picked up the parchment and read the words upon it, her heart racing as she did so.

B.O.B. – owl, she read, wondering what it meant.

"Excuse me," she said, as the peddler closed up the back of the wagon quickly and started to hitch it up to his horse. "Why were you selling blackberry pies today when you knew you shouldn't?"

"I only had the one," he told her, which sounded even stranger. "And I don't need you asking questions," he growled. He took off quickly, leaving the fair with a full wagon of different fruit pies though the festival had just started.

"Something is odd here," she said aloud. She looked at the note again, and then her attention was directed to Lord Henry speeding through the courtyard on his horse much too quickly with all the children and merchants around. He joined up with the man with the cart, nodded slightly, and then rode off ahead of him over the drawbridge and away from the castle.

"Lady Sapphire, what are you doing?" Lady Katherine made her way through the crowd and over to her, stopping twice to redirect her path as first several children ran in front of her and then a stray dog. "I have the steward taking your place in hiring, but I really wanted you to do it since you are to be the new lady of the castle soon."

"Oh, Lady Katherine, I think something bad is about to happen."

"What do you mean? And have you seen Henry?" Her chin raised and she scanned the crowded courtyard for her husband. "He took off so quickly, I didn't even get to say goodbye."

"He left with the pie vendor in a big hurry."

"The pie vendor? Whatever for?"

"He ate the cursed blackberry pie, my lady. And I saw him

take this from within it." Sapphire held up the small piece of parchment.

Lady Katherine looked at her quizzically. "That was in the pie? What does it mean?"

"I think we now have proof your husband is involved in the smuggling. I am sorry to say, but I believe this is someone telling him to meet at the Bucket of Blood, hence the B.O.B. The owl part – if I'm not mistaken, means the smugglers who call themselves Owlers."

"Then we need to go there to find out for certain," suggested Lady Katherine. "I want to know once and for all if my husband is involved in this or not."

"'Tis dangerous and I know Roe will not like it if he finds out. We were just starting to make amends for the last time I angered him by going to the tavern."

"Then don't tell him," she said. "That way if we are wrong, we'll not look foolish in his eyes or those of my husband's. I'll get the cloaks for us to hide under and you get our horses and we'll go anon."

"What about the hiring of the servants? And the fair? And what will Roe think when he gets back and I'm not here?"

"The steward can handle the hiring, and we will be back before Roe returns or before the fair is over. We'll just go to the tavern and watch from outside. We don't even have to go in. If we see Henry there then we'll know he is involved and we'll come back and tell Roe."

"All right," Sapphire agreed. "But I want to take Dugald with us so we're not unescorted. He can keep a secret, so we'll be fine."

"Then do it," instructed Lady Katherine. "But hurry. And make certain no one else knows where we've gone."

* * *

Roe hurriedly collected the taxes, surveyed the fields, and tended to the rest of his duties in the village. He was excited to get back to Sapphire and give her the dagger and tell her about the mysterious, old, blind hag. His duties as lord were taking much too long.

"We're done here." Roe looked over to his squire. "Let's get back to the castle."

They returned quickly and entered the busy bailey. Excitement coursed through him, thinking of the wonderful night he had planned to spend with his betrothed. He glanced over the courtyard, but didn't see her. Then he saw the steward and rode up next to him, with Waylon right behind him.

"Where is Lady Sapphire?" he asked.

"I am not sure, my lord. I haven't seen her all afternoon."

"I thought she was assisting my mother with the hiring of the servants."

"Nay, I did it by myself," explained the steward. "Your mother and Sapphire left early this afternoon, and to my knowledge they have yet to return."

"Left? In the middle of a festival and after she told me we needed to be here. Where did she go?"

"I'm not sure my lord. I was busy and didn't really pay attention. But all I know is that when Lady Sapphire saw Lord Henry heading over to the pie vendor, she followed him. She was mumbling something about a blackberry pie."

"What about it?"

"I don't know, but I do know Lord Henry seemed eager to eat it once he heard about it."

"This doesn't make sense."

Waylon interrupted just then. "Lord Sexton, while you were collecting the taxes, I thought I saw your stableboy ride by quickly. If I'm not mistaken, there were two women covered in cloaks with their hoods hiding their faces traveling with him."

"Sapphire," he said. "Who else would wear a hood in this blasted hot weather? In what direction were they headed?"

"Toward the docks," answered Waylon.

"Toward the docks?" repeated Roe. "I wonder where they were going and why."

"I know where they went, my lord." Erin rushed up to him having overheard their conversation. She had a frantic look upon her face.

"Erin, what's the matter?"

"Dugald told me not to tell anyone, but I just have to say something because they didn't come back and I am so worried."

"Who didn't come back? Are you talking about Sapphire and my mother?"

"Aye. They went to the Bucket of Blood Tavern."

"What the hell!" growled Roe. "I told her to stay away from there. What would possess her to do such a thing?"

"Dugald said she found a note in a pie or something. I don't know exactly, but I think it has something to do with the smuggling."

"Waylon, let's go get them."

"Aye, my lord."

"Let me come, too, Lord Sexton," pleaded Erin.

"Nay. 'Tis much too dangerous. Now just stay here and wait for our return, and I mean it."

Roe headed out of the castle with Waylon right behind

him. Suddenly his sweet thoughts of Sapphire he'd been having all day turned sour. With the anger he was feeling right now by her defying his orders, he knew she'd better say her prayers. And though he didn't eat of the devil pie, he still felt no better than the devil right now, because he wanted to kill her for betraying him yet again.

CHAPTER 19

Daughters of the Dagger

Sapphire stopped her horse just out back of the Bucket of Blood Tavern, noticing another horse that looked a lot like Lord Henry's. There was also the pie vendor's cart that now had no pies upon it, though she saw the man drive away with the wagon loaded down with them.

"He's inside, all right," said Lady Katherine. "And my heart aches to say this, but we need to go tell Roe."

"Well, mayhap he isn't really involved," said Sapphire, knowing better but wanting to comfort Lady Katherine. "Perhaps he just went in for a bite to eat."

"With the festival going on and with all the food the vendors were selling?" asked Dugald.

"Thank you, Lady Sapphire. I know you are trying to give me hope, but we just finished a large goose dinner," explained Lady Katherine. "He is not in there to eat. Now, let's go get Roe."

"Let's just make sure first," Sapphire protested. "Dugald, go inside and see what's going on."

"Me, my lady?" The boy looked as white as a ghost. She realized she'd put him in an awkward position.

"Then just stay here, and I'll go inside." Sapphire dismounted, preparing to go have a look for herself.

"Nay," protested Lady Katherine "'Tis too dangerous."

"I'll go," said Dugald bravely, getting off his horse.

"Just say you wanted to talk to Erin's father or that she needs something from him," instructed Sapphire.

"I will." The boy disappeared inside, and Lady Katherine dismounted and stood next to Sapphire as they patiently waited. After a short while, when Dugald did not return, Sapphire felt restless and anxious.

"Something's wrong, I just know it. I never should have sent him in there alone. I'm going in to get him," she announced.

"Not without me," said Lady Katherine, following close behind her as they made their way inside the establishment together.

"Dugald?" Sapphire called out softly, looking around the kitchen of the tavern. It was empty. Actually, she realized the tavern was closed today because everyone was at the festival at the castle. "I don't see him," she said, peering through the dark since the shutters were closed. "Do you?"

"Nay," said Lady Katherine, holding on to the back of her.

Then Sapphire's foot hit something on the floor, almost causing her to trip. She looked down and gasped when she saw Dugald prone on the floor and with a gash with blood flowing from his forehead.

"Nay! Dugald, are you all right? Please don't be dead," cried Sapphire, dropping to her knees to inspect the boy and his wound.

"Ohhh," Dugald moaned and opened his eyes.

"Thank God you're alive," said Sapphire, using the sleeve of her gown to wipe the blood from the boy's head, trying to stop the bleeding.

"What happened?" asked Lady Katherine. "Who did this to you, Dugald?"

"Only I am to blame," he said. "I walked in and overheard men talking about tuns of smuggled wool that they were planning on shipping out today. There is basically no one on the docks, as they are all at the castle for the festival. When the men came closer, I tried to hide, but tripped in the dark and hit my head on something."

Sapphire got up and found a cloth on the table and handed it to Lady Katherine.

"Please tend to his wound," she told her. "I am going to go find out what's going on."

"Nay," the woman protested. "Don't go. Let's just leave," she begged Sapphire.

"Can you ride?" Sapphire asked Dugald.

"I think so." Dugald tried to sit up and his eyes rolled back in his head. He slumped back down to the floor in Lady Katherine's arms.

"He's not going anywhere," said Sapphire. She thought she heard voices in the other room, but they were muffled. "I'll be right back," she whispered, heading into the main area of the tavern.

While the shutters were closed and 'twas dark, she could see candlelight coming from – of all places, the hearth that was never used. She ducked down and looked within realizing there was a secret door inside the back of the hearth that was partially open. The candlelight was coming from inside, and she could hear people talking.

"Bring the cart around to the Old Bell Inn. This tunnel leads right to it. And the rest of you – roll these barrels out through the passageway quickly. That festival won't last all day. We have already bribed the dockworkers by paying them more than we should. Before anyone knows what happened, we'll have our ship overseas and the delivery made."

It was the baron's voice. She was sure of it.

"After this, I don't want ye anywhere near my tavern, ever again. I didn't want to be a part of this in the first place and ye know it."

That had to be Auley O'Conner, she decided.

"If you want that little girl of yours to grow up to be an adult, you'll do as I say," threatened the baron.

"I don't like this either," came another voice. "I want no part of any of this after today either."

"You have no choice, you sot," snapped the baron. "You owe me for not only keeping your secret with the wine, but also suggesting you marry that bitch to ensure you get your brother's entire inheritance. If I must remind you, I was also the one who came up with the plan of me marrying the other bitch so you could keep half the earl's dowry instead of sending her packing. You benefitted greatly from all this. Too bad the little plan was ruined when your nephew decided to finally come home."

The baron was talking to Lord Henry. But their voices were getting muffled and Sapphire needed to get closer to hear more. She needed to open the door just a crack more if she wanted to gather all the evidence she needed. She ducked down into the enclosure of the hearth and put her hand on the secret door, preparing to push it open.

"There are some horses out back that weren't there before when I parked the cart," came a roughened voice that was probably the dockman that had posed as a pie vendor.

"Then go back out and see what's going on," grumbled the baron. "The rest of you get moving these barrels through the passageway to the Old Bell Inn. Urian will bring the cart around and load it up and take it down to the dock where we'll put it on the ship and set sail before anyone returns."

The secret door opened a tiny bit more and Sapphire was able to see the baron, the innkeeper, and Lord Henry, bent over as the earthen passageway was not all that high. The door squeaked as she moved it, and three heads turned to look at her.

"You!" shouted the baron. Sapphire tried to get away, but her foot tangled in her long gown and she fell when she tried to stand. A hand gripped her by the hair and pulled her to her feet. She came face to face with the man she despised as well as feared most in this world – Baron Lydd.

"I'll kill you for this, bitch," he shouted. Sapphire was suddenly reminded why she feared and hated him so much, when his fist slammed into her face and her world turned dark in front of her eyes.

"Roe," she heard herself calling out as she fell to the floor unconscious.

CHAPTER 20

*R*oe approached the Bucket of Blood Tavern, seeing that it was closed for the day and the shutters were covering the windows. There were no horses out front, nor did he see any movement down at the dock.

"She's not here," said Waylon, scanning the grounds from the top of his horse.

"I'll check out back and you ride down to the docks and see if there are any workers who may have seen them," commanded Roe.

"Aye, my lord." Waylon headed to the docks and Roe made his way to the back of the building. He had almost convinced himself that perhaps Erin was wrong after all and that Sapphire hadn't come here, until he saw three horses tied up out back in the thicket.

"Damn!" he spat, sliding from his horse and tethering it to a nearby tree. "Sapphire, why didn't you listen to me?" He looked down to the jeweled dagger at his waist and rubbed his hand over the hilt. He wanted more than anything to be back at the castle with Sapphire in his arms, safe and sound. He had a bad feeling in his gut about all this. Even before he stepped a foot inside, he knew whatever he found wasn't going to be good.

He pulled his sword from his sheath and stood with his back to the door, surveying the grounds around him. Then he pressed the latch and opened the door, stepping one foot inside, being led by the tip of his blade.

Something crashed down toward his head, but his hand shot up and he managed to keep from being hurt. He was ready to shove his blade into the person, when he turned to realize it was a woman.

"Mother!"

His mother dropped the pot with a clatter to the floor and embraced Roe.

"Oh, Roe I am so glad to see you."

"What are you doing here and where is Sapphire?"

He heard a moan and looked to the floor to see Dugald trying to sit up. He was holding a bloodied rag to his forehead.

"Dugald, what the hell happened to you?" he asked.

"I'm sorry, my lord. I only came along because I knew you'd want me to protect them."

"And a fine job you're doing, lying on the floor while my mother is fending me off with a damned pot. Now where the hell is Sapphire?"

"Katherine? What are you doing here?" Henry stepped out of the next room with a candle in his hand. He placed it on the table before noticing Roe. "This isn't what you think, Roe."

"And what would that be, Uncle? That you are a smuggler and a no-good lying bastard who took my mother to your bed just so you'd gain my father's inheritance?"

"Henry, please don't tell me you're a part of the smuggling," begged Lady Katherine.

"I'm sorry, sweetheart," said Henry shaking his head, "but I had no choice."

"That's right," said the baron, stepping into the room followed by Auley and half a dozen men. "He owed me for keeping quiet years ago for his cheating the king out of prisage. I was the one who caught him wanting to keep all the wine for himself."

"You did?" asked Katherine. "How could you?"

"I was on the wrong path before I met you," Henry explained. "But I wasn't going to do something like this again after this shipment, I promise you."

"What about you, Auley?" asked Roe. "I've known you forever. And I've always treated your daughter like a sister, and yet you resort to this?"

"He told me he'd kill Erin if I didn't help him. And since my tavern has the secret passageways, he needed to use them. I didn't have a choice," explained the innkeeper.

The door behind Roe opened and in walked not only his squire but also Erin.

"Father?" Erin said, looking at Auley questionably. Then Dugald moaned from the floor and she spotted him. "Dugald, nay!" She rushed over to him and fell to the floor, cradling him in her arms.

"Where's Sapphire?" Roe growled. "If you bastards did anything to hurt her, I swear I'll kill every single one of you."

"You'll never get that chance, Sexton," said the baron, motioning to his men. "Kill them all." His men pulled out weapons of swords, maces, and axes and rushed forward. Erin screamed and Roe's mother was frozen in fear.

"Over my dead body," shouted Roe. He lunged forward and took down a crazed man who was swinging a mace and rushing right for him. "Mother, get the hell out of here. Erin, you and Dugald do the same."

"There are too many of them, my lord," shouted Waylon, as he raised his sword and fought as well. Roe headed toward his mother to try to push her out the door, but a dockman got to her first, his dagger already being raised to her throat. Before Roe could even turn to help her, Henry rushed forward screaming, and grabbed the man from behind.

"You'll not touch my wife," he cried. The attacker turned and stabbed his dagger right through Henry's heart. Roe was fighting off two men at once but, from his side view, he saw Henry drop to his knees. The man pulled the dagger from Henry's chest, but before he could turn, Roe had taken him down by his own sword.

"Henry, nay!" His mother screamed and dropped to her knees, grabbing on to her dead husband. Dugald sat up, rubbing his head and when another man tried to swing a mace at Erin, he jumped up and grabbed the man and wrestled him to the ground.

Auley ran over with a sword in his hand and stabbed the man to death. "No one is going to harm my daughter. Ever again!" He looked over to the baron who was just standing in the doorway. "Ye've hit her and bruised her and I looked the other way and blamed it on the boy. But no more. I no longer care what happens to me, but ye'll not hurt my daughter again."

He lunged for the baron, but was blocked by another man.

"Dugald, get Erin and my mother the hell out of here,"

shouted Roe. "Get back to the castle and tell my knights what's going on. Send help at once."

"Aye, my lord." Dugald got to a standing position, staggering once. But with Erin's help, he made it to the door.

"Mother, go!" Roe shouted, knowing she was still lamenting over Henry. She got to her feet, crying and, thankfully, the three of them left. Roe could only hope they'd make it to safety before anything happened to them.

"I'm on yer side," said Auley, helping to fight off the men. "I know I'll be imprisoned for the rest of my life for this, but just make sure to take care of my baby girl."

"Where's Sapphire?" Roe shouted, realizing the baron had disappeared.

"She's in the other room. The baron hit her and she passed out," Auley told him.

"Nay!" Roe made his way through the dead bodies, leaving the last two men for Auley and Waylon to fight. He rushed into the room and looked around frantically, but didn't see her. "Sapphire," he called, but there was no answer. He felt the dread within him, realizing the baron had taken her. He had no idea where they'd gone, nor what would happen to her, but he knew he had to find her.

Waylon and Auley rushed in just then, holding their weapons high.

"Where'd he take her?" Roe asked Auley. Then grabbing the front of Auley's tunic, he almost lifted the man off his feet. "I said, where are they?"

"I don't know," answered Auley. "But I do know that these tunnels lead to the Old Bell Inn, where a cart is waiting to take the tuns of wool to the ship."

"What ship? Where?"

"We had one on the docks, and in case that plan was foiled, there is one waiting at Dungeness as well."

"Dungeness? There's no port there," said Roe.

"There's not, but there is a spot just off the tip where the ships can get close enough to load by using a small boat," explained Auley.

"Then show me the way through these tunnels," ordered Roe, ducking and entering in through the secret passageway through the hearth. "I only hope it's not too late because I have so many things to tell Sapphire. I love her and don't want to lose her."

Roe put his hand on the hilt of the jeweled dagger and rubbed it for luck. If superstitions were real, then he hoped the one of her finding her true love with the dagger was real because he needed more than anything to find Sapphire right now.

CHAPTER 21

Sapphire felt the movement of the cart beneath her even before she was able to open her eyes. Her head hurt like hell and the sleeve of her gown was covered in blood from wiping Dugald's forehead. She sat up, holding on to the side of the cart, being jostled back and forth as they rode much too fast over the rocky terrain.

"Keep your head down," came the baron's growl from the front of the wagon.

A man drove, and there were two more men inside the wagon with her, trying to tie down the barrels as they traveled. She figured these were the tuns containing the stolen shipment of wool. Half a dozen men rode on horses on both sides of them, and they all looked to be hired ruffians.

"Where are we?" she asked, gripping the sides of the wagon, feeling every bump like it was a blow from a mace.

"Your lover spoiled our little plan and now we have to move on to the alternate plan instead. Dammit, I knew something like this was going to happen. We would have gotten away by now if you hadn't poked your nose into it."

The baron sounded angrier than she'd ever heard him. And she knew that with his temper, it wasn't going to end well for her. Now she regretted going into the tavern in the first place and ignoring Lady Katherine's plea to go back to the castle and tell Roe. She only hoped that Lady Katherine and Dugald had managed to get away. She wanted to know, but was afraid to ask what happened to them. If he told her he'd killed them, she'd never forgive herself for her stupidity of going to the Bucket of Blood Tavern in the first place. Why hadn't she just stayed at the castle and obeyed Roe instead of being so curious and putting others in danger?

The baron reached over into the wagon and Sapphire anticipated his fist and moved quickly to the side. His fist smashed into the wood and blood splattered onto the front of her gown.

"Damn you, bitch. If I didn't want to collect the ransom on you, you'd be dead already. But by that sizable dowry you had, I'm sure there's much more I can get out of your father. Not to mention your lover. Once we're safely across the channel, I'll send a messenger back with my demands."

"You'll never get away with this," she cried. "Roe won't let you."

"Well, for all I know, he's already dead back at the tavern along with all your miserable friends."

"Nay, that's not true." Sapphire had to hold on to the belief that they were still alive. She refused to even think that they weren't.

"Well, now, I guess we won't know until we get to France and send the messenger with the ransom, will we?"

"I'll not go anywhere with you."

"You don't have a choice." He grabbed the reins from the driver and slapped the horse with them himself. "We need to go faster," he shouted.

They hit a bump and a barrel flew off the cart and smashed against the rocks, breaking open.

"Shall we stop and get it?" asked one of the men.

"Nay, leave it. We need to get to the ship before we're caught. I can only hope the partial shipment I sent to the docks will distract them enough and slow them down to enable us to get away."

Sapphire looked over the side of the cart and thought about jumping. Then she decided that would be no good. They were moving too fast. Even if she didn't kill herself with the fall, the baron would just come back and get her, beating her for her attempt to escape.

She noticed the shingled shoreline they now rode along. And while the rocks were all rounded, her soft slippers could not handle running on the stones.

She slipped back down into the wagon and closed her eyes and prayed. *Please, dear God, let Roe find me before it is too late.*

ROE MADE his way out of the tunnel with Waylon and Auley right behind him. They exited through a rotating cupboard inside the Old Bell Inn.

"That was amazing," said Waylon, in awe of how the tunnels led from one building to the next and all the way to the docks.

Roe was impressed as well. He had heard of things such as

this but had never experienced it himself. He thought this would come in handy if anyone inside was ever attacked.

"Now where?" he asked Auley, looking up and down the docks. They had exited right near the ships. The docks were still almost barren, as everyone was attending the festival at his castle. Right where he wanted to be – with Sapphire right now.

"The ship down at the end is ours," Auley said. "I see one of our men. Let me signal to him. Stay behind me, and mayhap we can catch them before they leave port." Auley let out the hoot of an owl, and was answered by another. "All right," he told them. "The coast is clear. No one should notice ye until ye're nearly on the ship."

"Go aboard and find out what's happening," said Roe. "And come back and tell us if the shipment and Sapphire are on board at all."

After the man left, Waylon questioned him. "Are you really going to trust him?"

"Well, the man's daughter is at my castle. If he truly cares for her like it seemed back at the inn, then yes, I trust he'll tell the truth."

They waited for a few moments, then Auley came back down the docks and to their hiding spot behind the Old Bell Inn.

"Sapphire's not here, nor is the baron," he told him. "There's only a few tuns here to distract ye. The rest of the shipment was taken to Dungeness where another ship awaits."

"Damn!" Roe had hoped they were here, as it would be easier to end all this nonsense right now. But now he'd travel well into the night to try to catch them in Dungeness. He only hoped he wouldn't be too late.

"How many men are aboard this ship?" asked Roe.

"Only half a dozen," the man relayed the information. "The rest of the men that the baron hired are either with him or already waiting at the ship in Dungeness."

"What does he want with Lady Sapphire?" asked Waylon.

"Probably a ransom, since he's a greedy son of a bitch," said Roe.

"Then let's go get her," said Waylon.

Roe looked over at Auley. He wasn't really sure he could trust the man fully yet, or he'd leave him here and take his squire. Nay, he decided, he didn't want to risk it. He'd have to keep an eye on Auley after all.

"Nay, Waylon, you stay here until the help arrives from the castle," Roe told him. "They should be here any time now. Have any man on that ship or involved in this smuggling thrown into the dungeon until my return."

"You're going to fight off the baron and his men yourself?" asked Waylon, not agreeing with Roe's decision.

"Send my soldiers to Dungeness after that," he instructed. "And in the meantime . . . Auley, you're coming with me."

"My lord, with all due respect, you might be taking a traitor with you who'll stab you in the back as soon as you turn around," Waylon warned him.

"I'm quite aware of that," Roe answered. "So that's why I tell you that if you find me dead, be sure to kill Erin."

"What? Nay," said Auley. "What if the baron kills ye after I'm already dead?"

"You'd better hope that doesn't happen. And you'd better fight your damndest to protect me as well as save Sapphire if you ever want to see your daughter again."

"My lord?" Waylon asked in astonishment as they headed back toward their horses.

"You heard me, Squire. If I die, kill this man's daughter." Then he turned his head so Auley couldn't see him and looked at Waylon and winked. Waylon nodded and smiled slightly, and Roe knew he'd just gained Auley's undying devotion and that the man would not betray him again.

CHAPTER 22

The wagon stopped abruptly, almost sending Sapphire crashing against the barrels. She looked out over the side and saw the ship docked on the tip of Dungeness.

All around her was a shingled strand, as no sand but only rocks made up the shores here. Small fishermen's shacks made of the driftwood from wreckage dotted the coastline. She noticed the fishing nets spread out across the hot stones, still drying in the setting sun.

Further inland was a boggy marsh. Grassland dotted with sheep covered the area as far as the eye could see. And at the edge of the Romney Marsh she could see the towers of Castle Lydd stretching up into the sky.

As they approached the ship, she noticed two shuttle boats pulled up onto the shore and a good dozen men waiting to load the tuns into the small boats to take them to the ship since there wasn't a dock. The barrels weren't that heavy since they were filled with wool, so the men were able to move them quickly over the shingles and into the docking boats.

But since the barrels were large, they could only fit in a few at a time.

"What about her?" asked one of the men with a nod of his head toward Sapphire. "Do you want her on the ship as well?"

"Leave her, as I'm the only one who knows how to handle the bitch," said the baron.

Sapphire knew what that meant. It meant that if she even tried to fight him or escape, he'd beat her. She couldn't outrun him on the stones and neither could she outfight him. Her hand went to her side, looking for her eating dagger, but he'd obviously removed it when he'd knocked her unconscious earlier. She had no choice now but to do as he said.

He pulled her from the wagon roughly, and she stumbled to the ground. Her hands hit the stones and scraped her skin.

"Get up, you clumsy wench," he commanded, pulling her up by the hair. She bit back the pain, not wanting to give the man the satisfaction of letting him know he'd hurt her. She looked down the road but didn't see help coming. The sun was setting and once it got dark, her chances of being saved would diminish quickly. Glancing back at the marsh with the sheep, she noticed two men who looked like Alice's brothers. She lifted her arm to signal to them, but the baron grabbed it and twirled her around.

"Stop it, you fool," he spat. "Don't you realize that if you call them over, they're only going to lose their lives?"

She hadn't thought about it but, now that he said it, she realized it was true. She didn't want anyone dying because of her, even if they were naught but sheepherders. Already, she'd endangered Lady Katherine and Dugald, and wasn't even sure if they were still alive. Roe would be in danger as well when he came to try to save her.

The baron started hauling her toward the ship when one of his men rode up to them from down the road, having been sent as a lookout.

"Two men approach on horseback," the man reported.

"Who are they?" asked the baron.

"I'm not sure, but one of them looks to be a knight."

"It's Roe! I told you he'd come for me." Sapphire felt a sudden surge of hope, and also concern. There was no way two men could fight off over a dozen. She needed to help him, but she didn't know what to do.

"How far off are they?" asked the baron.

"They were at the point where we lost the barrel, my lord."

"Then that means we have only a few minutes to set sail." The baron looked up at the ship but his men were still loading. Sapphire knew they didn't have time to finish and set sail before Roe made it to them.

"Shall we stop them, my lord?"

"Aye. Take two men with you down the road and hurry back. And don't fail me, do you understand?"

Sapphire watched the men ride down the road with their weapons drawn and could only hope for her sake as well as Roe's that they *would* fail.

* * *

ROE SLOWED his horse when he saw the broken barrel with wool scattered all over the ground. He stopped only for a moment, knowing they were on the right track.

"I see three men approaching," said Auley. "They are moving quickly, and with weapons raised."

"Then get your dagger ready and I hope to hell you are good with a blade."

"Not all that great," he said seeming very nervous.

Roe now wished for his squire at his side, thinking mayhap it was a mistake to take Auley along. But he'd wanted to keep an eye on the innkeeper and he needed Waylon to direct his soldiers to the men back at port. Well, he decided, this would be the true test of Auley's loyalty.

"Just remember," said Roe. "If I die, my squire has been given orders to kill Erin."

"Ye wouldn't do that," he said. "Ye are too fond of her. Ye told me yerself she's like a sister to ye."

"Do you feel lucky enough to test that theory?" he asked.

"Nay, my lord," he answered with a shake of his head.

"Then raise your damned weapon and fight to save your daughter's life."

He did as instructed and they rushed forward, meeting the three men head on.

* * *

SAPPHIRE SAT in the corner of the dark fisherman's hut with her back against the wooden wall of the shack and her hands and feet tied in front of her. The baron ripped off a piece of his tunic and used it to tie it around her mouth, making sure part of it was inside her mouth so she could not call out.

"You so much as mumble and I'll cut out your tongue," he warned.

She didn't think that was true, since she'd be worth more for ransom with her tongue intact, but she didn't want to risk it, so she stayed quiet and still.

"If your lover is not killed, then he'll come looking for you. The first place he'll look is on the ship. Since I can't sail before he gets here, I'm putting you in here for safe-keeping. Once he's on the ship, there's no way he can escape his death even with another man along. He's outnumbered. I'll slaughter him myself and then I'll come get you and we'll be on our way overseas. Now sit here like a good little girl until I return."

He reached out and grabbed her breast, making her jump. Then he lightly ran his hand over her cheek.

"I miss that body, believe it or not. I think I may just keep you for myself after all, even if you can't bear me an heir."

His finger came close to her mouth and though she was gagged, she bit down hard enough to make him jerk away from her.

She should have known the slap to her face was coming next, but still it was not as bad as having him touch her in a sexual way again. She hated this man more than anything. There was no way she could just sit here and let him get away with all this.

If Roe died today, then she might as well be dead, too. Because she would never forgive herself if he died from one of her foolish antics, nor would she want to live without him.

Once the baron left, she worked the ropes on her hands. When they didn't budge, she managed to turn around and kick at the side of the hut. She'd almost had the plank torn off when the door burst open behind her. She expected to find an angry baron, but instead she saw Alice, the baron's wife, standing there.

"Lady Sapphire, are you all right?" Alice hurried to her and took the gag from her mouth.

"Alice, you shouldn't be here. If the baron finds you, he'll kill you."

The woman pulled a dagger from her side and cut the ropes from first Sapphire's hands and then her feet.

"I was visiting my brothers on the marsh when they told me they'd seen you. I sent one of them to the castle upon horseback to get help. The other has signaled that there is trouble by blowing upon his sheep horn to warn everyone who hears it to come to our aid. Help should arrive shortly, so don't worry."

"Roe is on the road trying to save me," she said. "The baron just sent some of his men to kill him."

"Then let's see if we can be of any help. Now, come on and follow closely."

* * *

ROE WAS IMPRESSED by the way Auley fought, and knew now the man would truly risk his life in order to save his daughter. While Roe managed to take down two of the men, Auley did his part with the third.

They urged their horses faster toward the ship, but still being cautious. There would be more men than he could fight there, but still he had to try. For Sapphire's sake, he had to fight even if it meant his death.

"You're too late, Sexton." The baron walked up the beach with a dozen armed men behind him. "The ship is just about loaded and you have no chance of stopping me now."

"Where's Sapphire?" Roe ground out. "If you hurt her –"

"I'm here, Roe."

Roe turned to see Sapphire standing there with the baron's wife, Alice.

"What?" The baron was taken by surprise. "Alice, what are you doing here and why did you help her?" He headed closer to them.

"Because you're an evil man, Walter," Alice answered. "Lady Sapphire is not going to be hurt by you anymore and neither am I." Alice stood her ground with a sword in her hand. Sapphire had a dagger gripped in her fist. Roe figured the woman had given it to Sapphire, as the first thing the baron would have done was to take any weapons away from her.

The baron sidled closer to Sapphire, managing to reach out and pull her into his arms. She tried to raise her dagger to him, but he knocked it out of her hand and held his sword to her throat.

"Let her go," said Roe, his anger fueled, his heart thumping. Things were going from bad to worse.

"Drop your sword, Sexton, or she dies."

Then Sapphire did something that Roe never expected. She turned her head and bit the man's arm. He screamed out and loosened his hold slightly. Roe took the opportunity to lunge forward and pull Sapphire out of his arms. He quickly flung her away from the baron, all the while protecting her by holding his sword up should the baron move forward.

"Get behind me!" he shouted, his sword clashing with the baron's as the man attacked. He saw the baron's men rushing forward with their swords drawn and he knew that he and Auley could not outfight them. His life flashed before his eyes and all he could think of was what would happen to his beloved Sapphire.

Then Alice shouted out, "Attack." Roe saw fishermen and sheepherders appearing from inside or behind the wooden huts, and rising up out of the tall grass in the field. And then he heard more shouts and the sound of horses, and was surprised to see soldiers from the castle racing down the road as well.

"Good, my soldiers are here. Kill them!" shouted the baron, but Alice just let out a laugh.

"They answer to me now, Walter," she told him. "You haven't been back to the castle in months, and I told them all exactly where you've been and what you've been doing as well."

An all-out melee was in progress with the commoners fighting the baron's men with boards and rakes and any weapon they happened to have on them. Several of the fishermen took the ends of the net and managed to slow down some of the baron's men by throwing it over them and pulling them off their feet to the ground. Roe kept the baron at bay, and was surprised the man was so skilled with a sword. By the shape he was in, Roe had never expected it.

"Why did you do it?" Roe ground out. "You are a baron, you had more than you need. Why be so greedy?"

"Your uncle and I had a deal," he shouted.

"My uncle is dead," Roe told him. "So your deal is dead as well."

"Nay!" he cried. "He is to blame for all this. It was all his idea."

"We both know that's not true," said Roe. "You were blackmailing him and he had no choice but to go along with your requests trying to keep you quiet. That's why he let you marry Sapphire, so you'd not reveal his past. Before he died, he claimed he really wanted nothing to do with this smuggling."

"That's true," Sapphire said from behind him. "I heard your uncle as well as Auley say they wanted nothing to do with this smuggling – but the baron forced them to do it."

One of the baron's accomplices raced up behind Roe. If it hadn't been for Sapphire calling out to warn him, Roe might not have turned in time to raise his sword and do the man in.

"You bitch!" he heard the baron call out. "If you hadn't turned my castle against me, I'd be across the sea by now." The baron's sword sliced through the air right toward Alice. Roe was too far away to help her, but Auley stepped in between Alice and the baron with his dagger lifted to block his blow. His weapon was knocked out of his hand and his shoulder sliced as well. Roe knew Auley was about to die and, in one move, he rushed forward and plunged his sword through the baron's heart.

"You've hurt and killed enough people," he ground out. "This stops now."

Sapphire screamed and he turned to see a dockman headed for her. He pulled his sword from the baron's chest, and lunged forward to stop the man, taking him down as well.

"Sapphire," he said, pulling her to him in a one-armed protective hold, keeping his sword raised should anyone else think to attack.

With the soldiers from the castle now there to help, Roe shouted out to the baron's smugglers who were left. "Drop your weapons and surrender. There is no way you can win now."

When they saw their fearless leader dead on the ground, they did as ordered.

Sapphire clung to Roe and cried softly.

"It's over now, sweetheart," Roe told her, trying to regain his breath from the fight.

"Roe, I'm so sorry for everything. I wish I could have fought and helped you, but I am not skilled with a weapon."

"Nor do I expect you to be," he answered. "I am the one who will protect you, always."

He kissed her atop the head and pulled her into his embrace, never wanting to let her go. He'd almost lost her today, and this scared him more than any battle or war he'd ever fought. "You're safe now, Sapphire," he reassured her.

"Can we go home now?" she asked, her body shaking in his arms.

"Aye," he said, liking the way that sounded. "You are safe now and we are going home. And no one is ever going to harm you again."

CHAPTER 23

*S*apphire was so upset by what just happened, that the only thing that could stop her body from shaking was being wrapped in Roe's protective arms as she rode on the horse in front of him back to Castle Rye. She'd never been in the midst of a battle before and couldn't get the image of the dead and bloodied men from her mind.

They rode in silence back to the castle, neither of them feeling much like talking. Auley followed right behind them on his own horse. His shoulder was wrapped, thanks to Alice, and she followed on a horse with two of her guards alongside. Some of Roe's knights had met him on the road, and returned with them as well.

Roe and Alice had spoken before they left. The dead bodies, as well as that of the baron's, were being buried back at Lydd by the soldiers from the castle. The smugglers who had surrendered were being taken back to the dungeon at Lydd for now, and the wool was returned to the sheepherders who were very glad to have it back in their possession.

They rode through the castle gates late that night.

Sapphire could see the remains of the festival littering the courtyard. Her heart ached that she'd missed the celebration, as she really wanted to participate as well as get to know the people since she was going to be the new Lady Rye. Still, she had Roe to thank that she was alive, and wondered how Lady Katherine was faring. Roe had told her that Lord Henry had been killed in the tavern protecting her, but that Lady Katherine, Erin, and Dugald had escaped. Sapphire could only hope they had made it back to the safety of the castle.

The mood was sullen, but once inside the gates, the energy was different. Everyone cheered at their return. Roe's squire, Waylon, rushed over to take the reins of the horse.

"My lord, I am happy to see that you and Lady Sapphire are alive and well."

"Aye," said Roe. "I am happy to say we've not only stopped the smugglers and returned the goods, but stopped the baron as well."

"I hope he's dead!" Lady Katherine rushed over the cobbled stones to greet them. Roe dismounted and his mother hurled herself into his arms.

"Roe, thank God you are alive," she said, covering his face with kisses.

"I am fine, Mother," he told her, breaking the embrace to save himself from the embarrassment of being kissed further. "And, aye, the baron is dead."

"Sapphire," said Lady Katherine, coming to her side. "I am happy to see you are alive and unharmed as well."

"And I, you," said Sapphire with a smile. "I am alive thanks to your son," she told her. "Without him, I'd either be dead or across the sea with the baron right now, as he planned on ransoming me."

Roe reached up and helped Sapphire dismount. That's when she saw something she hadn't noticed before. On his waistbelt was fastened an ornate dagger with a blue sapphire gem in the hilt.

"Where did you get that?" she asked, pointing to the dagger. A newfound excitement rushed through her, making her feel alive.

"Oh, I nearly forgot." Roe unfastened the dagger and handed it to Sapphire. "This is a betrothal present for you, Sapphire. I got it at the fair from an old blind hag, and haven't had the chance to give it to you."

"This is my dagger!" she cried out.

"I thought you would like it, as it sounds similar to the dagger you told me you once had."

"Nay, not similar," she said, inspecting it. "It is the exact same one!"

"Sapphire, you lost that dagger close to two decades ago. How could that possibly be the same one?" asked Roe.

"You said you bought it from an old blind hag?"

"Well, she wouldn't let me pay for it. She said it was her contribution, and just gave it to me."

"Did she say anything else?" asked Sapphire.

"She was rattling on, asking me all kinds of questions about how much I loved you."

"What did you tell her?"

"I told her I loved you, Sapphire, and that is the truth. I love you more than anything and can't wait until we are married."

"It was her," said Sapphire, remembering the story her mother had told her of buying the daggers from the blind old hag. "It was the same lady my mother bought the daggers from in the first place, I am sure of it."

"That's impossible," said Roe. "If the blind hag was from Blackpool, how would she get all the way to Rye, as she is blind? Besides, she'd be so old she'd be dead by now, as that was many years ago."

"I don't know how or why, but I do know it was her. Don't you see? This dagger proves that you are my true love and we were meant to be together. Roe, I am so happy," she said, running her hand over the hilt of the dagger. "My dagger has come back to me after all these years, and my dream has come true. I have found my true love in you, and this has only verified it."

"Father, you are alive!" Erin ran out of the stable with Dugald right behind her. Auley jumped off the horse and his daughter barreled into his arms. He moaned and Erin realized he was wounded.

"You're wounded," she said, looking at his arm. "Tell me you'll be all right."

"I'll live," the man said with a large smile.

"He was injured when he saved my life," said Alice, slipping from her horse. Her guards stayed mounted atop their own horses.

"Erin, this is Alice," Auley said. "She is the Baroness of Lydd."

"Pleased to meet you," Erin said with a curtsy.

"So – are you the baron's wife?" asked Dugald.

"I was married to the wretched man," Alice admitted, "but I must say I only did it to ensure that my brothers and the rest of the sheepherders' land would be safe for them to continue raising the sheep for wool."

"What's going to happen to you, Father?" asked Erin. The girl's eyes teared up and opened wide as she looked directly at Roe. "You aren't going to have him punished for smuggling, are you, Lord Sexton?"

ROE'S HEART went out to the girl. He couldn't stand the fact that he was the one who was going to have to sentence her father.

"I'm sorry, Erin, but your father did some things that were very wrong."

"He was forced into it by the baron," said Erin. Then she looked at Auley and said, "Tell them father."

"It is true," the man said. "I did it only to ensure yer safety, Erin. But still, there was no excuse for being a part of the smuggling. Lord Sexton has every right to sentence me as he sees fit, so please don't be angry with him. Even if I go to my death for this, at least I will die knowing that ye are safe now, and have Dugald to watch over ye and protect ye."

"Auley saved my life," Alice spoke up, glancing at the man fondly. "I do think that should count for a lighter sentence."

"That's true," piped in Roe's mother. "After all, she is a baroness. That action needs to be rewarded. Too many people have died already over this, Roe. Henry was pulled into the baron's scheme as well. Although I realize he wasn't very honest or loyal, we did become very fond of each other. He went to his death protecting me. I'd be dead right now if it wasn't for him. Auley is the girl's father, so please don't take him from her. She doesn't deserve that."

"He knows smuggling is a punishable crime, though

usually not death on the first offense. Usually a hand is cut off to prove a point," Roe reminded them all.

"Nay!" cried Erin, gripping on to her father.

"It's all right, Erin," Auley said. "I deserve whatever punishment Lord Sexton gives me. Even without a hand, at least we'll still have each other."

"What are you going to do, Roe?" asked Sapphire. "Do you need to hold a trial?"

Roe hated being in this position. But as Lord of Rye, it was his decision how to handle the situation. He wanted more than anything to let Auley go without repercussions, but he had to uphold the rules and set an example for his people.

"I can't let you keep the Bucket of Blood, Auley," he told him.

"I understand," the man said with his eyes fastened to the ground in shame.

"However, I do think the inn would be a good wedding present to Dugald and Erin, don't you?"

"What?" he asked, looking up, hope back in his eyes. "Aye, I think so, too."

"Erin already knows how to run the place," Roe said. "But both she and Dugald are still young, so I will pay for an experienced man to help them until they are able to do it on their own."

"Thank ye, my lord. Ye are too generous," said Auley with a nod.

"What about my father?" asked Erin, with tears in her eyes. "Lord Sexton, what is going to happen to him?"

"Don't worry, I will not cut off his hand," Roe told her. "And since Auley did fight against the baron and his men, he has proved his loyalty to me and that I can trust him. Auley, you will not be sentenced. However, I will have to banish you from Rye forever."

"Nay," cried Erin. "I want to live near my father."

"Then I'll take him to Lydd," offered Alice. Auley smiled at her slightly, and Roe could see an exchange of admiration between the two of them. "That way he will be close enough for you to come visit him, Erin."

"But he still won't be able to come to Rye to see me," complained Erin.

"It's all right, sweetheart," said Auley.

"I'll make the exception for Auley to be able to visit Rye but only if accompanied by the baroness or one of the castle guards," said Roe. "And only twice a year, no more."

"Thank ye," said Auley with gratitude in his eyes.

"Aye, thank you," Erin echoed.

Roe looked across the courtyard, spying the dead body of his uncle lying in a wagon of hay. "I am sorry about your husband," he said to his mother. "He will be buried in the graveyard behind St. Mary's in the village alongside my father."

"What's going to happen to the dockmen who the baron bribed to help him?" asked Waylon.

"I know they were probably just victims of the baron and have families to feed as well," said Roe. "But still, they cannot go unpunished. They will do their time in the dungeon and, after that, I will send them overseas to fight for the king rather than having them sentenced to death. When I feel they have served sufficient time, they can return to their families, though they, too, will be exiled from Rye."

Sapphire was quiet, and he noticed she was still looking at

her dagger. He pulled her closer in a hug, remembering she had told him that she missed her family.

"I think the wedding banns have been posted long enough," he said, causing her to look up with question in her eyes.

"What do you mean, Roe?"

"I mean, I cannot wait another moment to marry you. So in the morning, a missive will be sent to your father and sisters asking them to come to Rye anon. And as soon as they arrive here, you and I will be married."

"I'd like that," said Sapphire, her eyes twinkling in the firelight from the night torches of the castle. "And I want more than anything in the world to be your wife. Because although I knew it before, I am now convinced." She held her dagger up for him to see. "I have found my true love in you."

CHAPTER 24

'$\mathcal{T}$was less than a sennight later, and the day of the wedding was here. Sapphire waited nervously in the courtyard, pacing back and forth waiting for her father and twin sisters as they had yet to arrive, though their messenger had said they'd be here this morning.

"Calm down," said her sister, Ruby, who had arrived last night with her husband, Lord Nyle Dacre. "You are so nervous that you are making the baby jump."

"Really?" Sapphire surveyed her sister dressed in a golden gown with the bulge of the baby very noticeable now. Her hair was so light blond that it was almost white. With the sun shining down upon her, she looked like an angel.

"Give me your hand," said Ruby, "and you'll see for yourself."

Ruby reached out and took Sapphire's hand, placing it on her stomach. The baby kicked and Sapphire felt it beneath her fingers. She jumped back and pulled her hand away quickly.

"Oh!" she cried out.

"You act as if you think the baby is going to bite you," said Ruby with a giggle.

Sapphire giggled, too, when she realized her sister was right. It felt so good to have Ruby here that Sapphire couldn't stop smiling. They both laughed and hugged, as Ruby's husband walked up to meet them.

"What is the laughter all about?" asked Lord Nyle Dacre.

"I'm just happy," said Sapphire. "And I can't wait to have a baby. Many of them!"

Roe joined them just then, overhearing what she said.

"That's fine with me," he agreed. "But just one at a time, all right? I know you have twin sisters and I am not sure if my ears could handle two babies crying at once."

"I'll take three at a time if I can get it!" exclaimed Sapphire, causing odd looks on both the men's faces. Ruby and Sapphire burst out laughing at that.

"A traveling party is arriving," announced Waylon coming to join them. "Lady Sapphire, I believe 'tis your father and sisters."

"Let's go." Sapphire took Ruby by the hand and they both took off running across the courtyard.

"Papa!" Sapphire cried out, almost pulling the man off his horse as he tried to dismount.

"Sapphire, I am so glad to be here." He gave her a hug and then acknowledged Ruby. "That baby looks like it'll be a good sized one. Congratulations, Ruby."

"Papa, don't say it that way or you'll make me feel like a whale. But thank you and it is good to see you."

Sapphire introduced her father as well as her twin sisters, Amber and Amethyst, to Roe and his mother. When everyone had exchanged pleasantries, Roe spoke up.

"Father Geoffrey awaits us at St. Mary's church. So if you would all join us on this special day, I do believe it is time for our wedding."

Sapphire ran her hand over the dagger at her waist, and her father spotted it.

"That looks familiar," he told her. "Did your dagger mysteriously show up just like it did with Ruby?"

"From a blind old hag as well," said Sapphire.

"Papa, mayhap we can find this old hag," said her sister, Amethyst. "I would really like to find not only my dagger but my true love as well." Amethyst had dark shoulder-length hair and a liveliness about her that was admired by all. She was always in a happy mood and enjoyable to have in one's presence.

"Where is the old woman?" Sapphire's father, Earl Blackpool, asked.

"We don't know," said Sapphire. "After Roe got the dagger from her, she seemed to disappear."

"What about you, Amber?" asked Ruby. "Don't you want to find your dagger and true love as well?"

"We'll see," Amber answered. Sapphire thought she was acting oddly. Though she was the quieter of the twins and always proper, she seemed to be holding a secret within. Sapphire knew Amber well enough to realize that she wouldn't say anything about what was on her mind until she was good and ready.

"Well, let's go to the church," Roe said. "I have a woman to marry and I can wait no longer."

"Me neither," said Sapphire, smiling and running a hand over the hilt of her dagger thinking how lucky she was to be marrying Roe and no longer being married to the horrible baron.

* * *

ROE STOOD at the top of the stairs of St. Mary's church, feeling like the luckiest man in the world. He looked over to Sapphire, just as they were getting ready to say their vows, drinking in her beauty.

It was custom to be married in blue, and she wore her bright blue velvet gown laced in gold trim. Her long, mahogany hair was braided loosely, trailing down her back. She wore a headdress composed of a metal circlet woven with bright red poppies and purple larkspur that she and Ruby had picked from the field outside the castle just that morning. A small veil was attached to the back. And on her neck she wore the sapphire necklace that had been her mother's. She also wore the sapphire jeweled dagger at her waist.

Ruby stood at her side and her twin sisters were right next to her.

Waylon stood at Roe's side, holding the sapphire ring that had been Sapphire's mother's. It was the ring that meant something to her. At her request, Roe was using this for the marriage.

"Repeat after me," the priest said. Roe took Sapphire's hands in his as they said their vows.

Roe glanced down the steps and saw his mother smiling at him and he only wished his father could have been here for this special day. Auley, with his injured shoulder wrapped, was there by Roe's permission. He noticed that the man and Alice were getting along wonderfully. Dugald stood with his arm around Erin, both of them beaming with bright smiles. Roe realized they were probably thinking of their own wedding right now.

Sapphire's father smiled and nodded to Roe in silent communication, relaying that he approved of the union.

"The ring, please," said the priest. Roe turned and took it from his squire.

Then he placed it upon Sapphire's finger, with some words of his own. "With this ring, I thee wed," he said. "And I promise to love and protect you for as long as we live. I love you, Sapphire. I will see to it that from this day forth you are treated as the princess that you truly are in my heart."

"I love you, Roe, and promise to honor and obey and be your true love for as long as we live," answered Sapphire.

"I pronounce you man and wife," said the priest. He didn't need to tell them to kiss, because Roe couldn't wait. He kissed Sapphire long and deep and then picked her up in his arms and twirled her in a full circle, making her laugh.

Placing her on her feet, they walked down the stairs with everyone tossing seed and grain in a shower of appreciation. It was a superstition to bring about a fruitful marriage with lots of children.

Waylon walked up next to him and tossed a handful of grain directly at Roe. "I've been waiting to do that," he said with a smile. "It's the only day when a squire can throw something at his lord and not be punished for it."

"Well, that's not really true," Roe told him. "And all I can say is I hope you enjoy sweeping it all up when you've finished."

Waylon laughed, then stopped and looked at Roe curiously. "You are jesting, aren't you?"

"I jest with you not. I won't have precious grain and seed fed to the birds when we will need it to plant in the fields come spring."

Waylon grumbled and the crowd laughed.

"Congratulations," the earl said, clasping arms with Roe. Then he hugged Sapphire as well.

"So, who will be the next to wed?" asked Sapphire, looking at her twin sisters, Amber and Amethyst. "Papa, have you betrothed either of them yet?"

"Nay," he admitted. "I've been informed of your ordeal with the baron and I have decided to stop betrothing my daughters. It was the dying wish of your mother. I will let Amber and Amethyst find husbands on their own."

"Well, I think I may have to look farther than Blackpool or Rye for my husband," said Amethyst. "I might just travel the lands to find my true love."

"What about you, Amber?" Sapphire asked the other twin. "Where will you look for your true love?"

"I do not have to look, as I have already decided," she said.

"Really?" Roe could see the excitement on Sapphire's face as she waited for her sister's answer. "Do tell us, please," Sapphire continued.

"I have decided to join the abbey and become a nun," announced Amber, causing everyone to suddenly become quiet. The mood changed from happiness to bewilderment instantly.

"Amber, are you sure?" asked Ruby, rubbing her belly. "If you do that, you will never be able to have children."

"I will atone for the sins of our mother as well as our entire family," explained Amber. "I have decided to join the Order and nothing any of you can say will change my mind."

"Amber, please reconsider," begged Sapphire. "You don't understand how it feels to find your true love."

"There is no man for me," she said. "Now please, just accept my decision."

"We are happy for you," said Roe, trying to make it more comfortable for the girl. "Everyone's path in life is different and we hope you find what you are looking for."

Everyone congratulated her then. And though he knew Sapphire – the woman who wanted a big family and liked to nurture and be a mother to everyone – would probably never understand, she smiled and gave her sister a hug of congratulations as well.

"Thank you, Roe," said Amber, her huge, round, green eyes smiling as she nodded. "I am happy for you and Sapphire. You have found a wonderful woman who will be the best mother ever."

Ruby cleared her throat and Amber laughed and added, "along with Ruby – and someday Amethyst as well."

"I agree she will make a wonderful mother," said Roe. "And I can't wait to start raising a family with my beautiful wife. For I, too, have married my true love and I now believe in the superstition told by the old hag. As a matter of fact, I will never doubt a superstition again, because I have living proof of finding true love by being married to one of the **Daughters of the Dagger – Sapphire.**"

FROM THE AUTHOR

I hope you enjoyed Sapphire and Roe's story. Through my research, I've discovered that during this time period, England cornered the market on fine wool trade. Because of the king's harsh taxes on overseas trade, and his control over supply and demand, smugglers often came into play. There truly were taverns and businesses that had secret passageways that connected to each other that were used for smuggling. I believe some of these buildings still exist today.

The third book in the **Daughters of the Dagger Series**, *Amber* explores the power as well as the corruption of the church in medieval times. You will follow Amber and Lucas on a pilgrimage and see the importance and beliefs they held of holy relics, as well as get a taste of life in a medieval monastery. And in *Amethyst*, my heroine has been sent to help build a castle for the border lord, Marcus Montclair.

Daughters of the Dagger Series:
  Prequel

Ruby – Book 1
Sapphire – Book 2
Amber – Book 3
Amethyst – Book 4

This is followed by my Scottish **Madman MacKeefe Series**, with the first book being about the girls' brother, *Onyx – Book 1*, who they thought was dead.

Aidan – Book 2, is next, followed by *Ian – Book 3.*

Thank you,

Elizabeth Rose

ABOUT ELIZABETH

Elizabeth Rose is a multi-published, bestselling author, writing medieval, historical, contemporary, paranormal, and western romance. Her books are available as EBooks, paperbacks, and audiobooks as well.

Her favorite characters in her works include dark, dangerous and tortured heroes, and feisty, independent heroines who know how to wield a sword. She loves writing 14th century medieval novels, and is well-known for her many series.

Her twelve-book small town contemporary series, Tarnished Saints, was inspired by incidents in her own life.

After being traditionally published, she started self-publishing, creating her own covers and book trailers on a dare from her two sons.

Elizabeth loves the outdoors. In the summertime, you can find her in her secret garden with her laptop, swinging in her hammock working on her next book. Elizabeth is a born storyteller and passionate about sharing her works with her readers.

Please visit her website at **Elizabethrosenovels.com** to read excerpts from any of her novels and get sneak peeks at covers of upcoming books. You can follow her on **Twitter, Facebook, Goodreads** or **BookBub.** Be sure to sign up for her

newsletter so you don't miss out on new releases or upcoming events.

ALSO BY ELIZABETH ROSE

Medieval

Legendary Bastards of the Crown Series

Seasons of Fortitude Series

Secrets of the Heart Series

Legacy of the Blade Series

Daughters of the Dagger Series

MadMan MacKeefe Series

Barons of the Cinque Ports Series

Second in Command Series

Holiday Knights Series

Highland Chronicles Series

Medieval/Paranormal

Elemental Magick Series

Greek Myth Fantasy Series

Tangled Tales Series

Contemporary

Tarnished Saints Series

Working Man Series

Western

Cowboys of the Old West Series

And more!

Please visit http://elizabethrosenovels.com

Elizabeth Rose

CPSIA information can be obtained
at www.ICGtesting.com
Printed in the USA
LVHW112211080921
697407LV00015B/193